The Marriage Trifecta

The Marriage Trifecta

By

Shelley O'Hara

Copyright © 2000 by Shelley O'Hara

All rights reserved.
No part of this book may be reproduced, stored in a retrieval system, or transmitted by any means, electronic, mechanical, photocopying, recording, or otherwise, without written permission from the author.

ISBN: 1-58721-356-7

1stBooks - rev. 4/17/00

About The Book

The Marriage Trifecta tells the story of a grandmother, Chantilly (Tilly for short), and her granddaughter, RaeAnn. Tilly sets up the Marriage Trifecta, a sort of raffle in which the family and friends of RaeAnn try to guess the month, year, and groom of her wedding. RaeAnn gets advice on all aspects of married life from each person, including Tilly ("marriage is like two mules in a harness"), her father (In a love letter to her mother: "Forgot to pick up my paycheck. But all I need is your love. By the way, I've been constipated for 165 days."), and her married best friend Samantha ("We never have sex, and when we do have sex, the theme to 'Rawhide' keeps running through my head.")

Will RaeAnn be an Old Maid? Or will Tilly successfully find a husband that suits not only RaeAnn, but her nutty family.

If you have an eccentric uncle or a mother that says any outrageous thing she thinks of, you'll enjoy this book. It's love and family so close to home you'll swear these people are your relatives.

Dedication

In memory of Mildred E. Gerdt

Chapter 1

The Marriage Trifecta

My grandmother, Chantilly McDaniel, went on a senior citizen trip to the racetrack in Cincinnati, met this old guy who taught her how to figure the odds, and set up the Marriage Trifecta, a sort of raffle in which my family and friends tried to guess the month, year, and groom of my wedding. Like a bookie, she'd figure the odds and pay-off for any number of combinations of husbands and wedding dates. She'd update the chart as I acquired and discarded new prospects. Practically everyone I knew had a stake in the Marriage Trifecta. The first I heard of this wagering on my future was at my other grandmother's funeral.

"I guess they'll just have to pack her in ice," my mom said when a snowstorm delayed us from traveling to my grandmother's funeral. "I can't help it if she picked the middle of a blizzard to die."

My mother Darla, my sister Lynne, my brother-in-law Harry, my nieces, Tilly and I, were all traveling up to my dad's mother's funeral in my sister's van. Bleary eyed and armed with tissues, we all looked as if we'd be sobbing for miles when actually we all had the same terrible cold. Mom was the worst. My brother-in-law, who is a pharmacist, had given her a concoction called Three-In-One that he made for her cough, and now she couldn't hear. Everything she said she screamed as if she were talking to a foreigner.

My sister looked upon the funeral as a vacation. She'd made reservations at the most expensive hotel, the only one in town with an indoor pool. She had stocked the van with rafts, cheese balls, cooler, peanuts, three suitcases for her portion of the family, a coffee can, and her living room couch. Because the van had only a driver and passenger seat, she actually did bring her living room couch. Also, it was Lynne's policy not to stop when traveling, so she made us all pee in a coffee can, even

Tilly. There was nothing like baring your ass and hearing the toot-toot of an approaching semi-driver. Tilly, Mom and I sat drinking beer and confessing aloud relief that Grandma Jess had died before her nursing home bills consumed all the family money.

"I know it's terrible, but at least I'm honest," Lynne called from the back of the van. "I'm glad she finally died and left Daddy at least a little of the money."

"I bet the first thing Daddy buys is a big boat," I said. "I hope there's enough left for a big boat."

"At least I'm relieved," Tilly said. "At least I'll know you all won't be crying and sobbing and feeling blue. Instead, you'll be drinking Budweisers and fighting over my diamond rings. Well, piss on you all. I want to be buried with them."

"I wonder who'll do the funeral for Jess," Mom said.

"Has Grandma ever been to church?" I said.

"Not that I know of."

"I hope Daddy remembers that Grandma wanted a closed casket," Lynne said.

"Actually, you're hoping that Daddy remembered the last time we visited Grandma she said 'Be sure Lynne gets my rings,'" I said.

"Speaking of rings," Tilly said, "isn't it about time you got one on your finger?"

She looked at me and pointed to her finger. At the time I didn't know what she was talking about. I just nodded.

"Jess never did like you, RaeAnn," Mom said. "You reminded her too much of me."

"She like me, though," said Lynne.

Lynne hadn't been up to visit since my mother had, which had been several years. "I don't think we'll go this time," they said to my dad. But I, for reasons unknown, always felt compelled to go. I had been the one to faithfully visit Jess in the nursing home, the one that wrote her letters, the one that sat wide awake in our old bedroom at the farmhouse while truck headlights sent visions of murderous hitchhikers dancing in my head.

The last time I went to visit Jess, her rear end started hurting, and she hollered at the top of her lungs, "My butt, my butt, my butt." The nurses ignored her, my dad blew air through his mustache and asked me if I was ready to leave, and I tried to comfort Jess.

"What can I do?" I asked frantically.

"My butt," she screamed in my face. And then in a normal, friendly conversational tone, she said, "When I die, be sure Lynne gets my rings."

When news came of Jess's death, we were more relieved than upset. Jess had diabetes, but she drank Pepsi and ate sugar cookies until a series of strokes confined her to a wheelchair. Her arm crimped up like a twisted, gnarled, piece of driftwood, light and useless. Her legs and mind withered up too, until all she could do was blink her eyes and say "Jeepers."

My grandfather, Louie, cared for her, leaving her at the big, oak dining room table, blinking and tapping her good hand until he came home from drinking all day at the Swizzle Stick with a piece of cold fried chicken for her supper. She'd smile at him and say, "Jeepers."

When my grandfather died, we put Jess in a nursing home, where she got her hair done once a week and had her own remote-controlled TV. Still, she declined so much, became as useless as her driftwood arm, that we thought her better off dead, sighed and said it was for the best when her time did come. Still, any funeral is difficult.

"You look more and more like your mom," my grandmother's sister, Aunt Celina said as I entered the funeral showing. "Although it's been so long since we've seen you."

Aunt Celina, although she had had four husbands, one of which died by mysteriously choking on an apple core, was the blame placer on Daddy's side. She gave me an accusing look and a little push. "Go see how nice your grandmother looks," she said.

My knees started to buckle, and I smiled weakly. I have a

loathsome fear of dead people—they look all waxy and pale. My knees knocked and hot spit, the kind that precedes vomiting, ran through my mouth. The thing I hated most about funerals is when people peered in the casket and said, "She looks so nice. They did a good job," like it was floral arrangement. When Tilly's sister Katie died, her niece picked out an orange polyester suit for her to be buried in. Her wig was crooked, and her lipstick was smeared all around her lips. Every time someone said she looked nice, I cringed. I could hardly look at her because that was not the Katie I knew. I didn't really want to take a look at Jess, but my mom came over and guided me up to the casket.

"Jess would just shit," Mom said loudly. Aunt Celina glanced our way. "Why I wish Jess would sit up and spit on Celina."

Aunt Claire and Aunt Celina were both watching us now. I jabbed my mom with my elbow and told her to hush. My mom didn't like my aunts, and my aunts didn't like my mom. Mom's comments wouldn't have been so bad except that she was yelling them. She thought she was whispering.

"Jess wanted a *closed* casket, but Celina insisted on an open casket. I just wish she'd sit up and at least point a finger at Celina or something."

We both stared down at Jess looking like a wax banana in a blue satin-lined casket. As I looked at her, all I could think of was Clark Gable and strawberry pies. Jess had the biggest crush on Clark Gable. The only time she acted silly, girlish even, was when a Clark Gable movie was on. She'd giggle and practically swoon as she watched it. I remembered that and her strawberry pies. She made the best strawberry pies in the world—no packaged gel or store-bought strawberries. Everything was made from scratch, and the strawberries were fresh from the garden. I was sad that I would never have another of her strawberry pies. Clark Gable reminded me of another thing about my grandmother.

"Her mustache is hardly noticeable," I said.

My mom glared at me, and her hand involuntarily reached for her upper lip. My grandmother had a pretty big mustache, and I could not bear to kiss her. Luckily she wasn't the affectionate type that screamed come here and insisted you give her a big wet kiss. In fact, she probably didn't want to kiss me either.

My dad also has a mustache. He shaved his off once, and we all swore part of his upper lip went along with the whiskers. His face just sunk where his upper lip should be perched, and we called him Andy Gump. He let it grow back and has kept it ever since. With a mustache, he looked fine. He looked like, well, like Grandma.

I spied my dad across the room talking with Aunt Madeline. His eyes pleaded for a rescue, so I walked over and put my arms around him.

"Well, RaeAnn," Aunt Madeline said. "You look just like your mother."

She clearly did not intend this to be a compliment, but I said thank you anyway.

"I hear you're getting married," she said.

I looked at my dad, and he shrugged.

"Jess looks wonderful don't you think," Madeline continued. "So natural." She clearly isn't looking at the same Jess I am. She's looking around the room. "Why there's Fern and Chuck from my Bridge Club. I must go say hello."

The sight of Fern and Chuck perked Madeline up a bit, but before she joined her fellow bridgees, she unclasped her purse, extracted a hanky, squeezed and squinted her eyes until a tear appeared in one corner, and then, finally, she left us to join her friends.

Lynne appeared. "Who are all these people?" she said. "I don't know any of them."

"They're friends of Celina's and Claire's," Mom said, scooting in behind Lynne. "Thank God they came to fill this place up. If they didn't, who'd be here?"

"Just us," I said.

"And I bet they were wondering if we'd show," Mom said.

"Shhh," Lynne said. "You talk too loud."

"Why I'm barely whispering," she hollered. "I can hardly hear myself."

"That's because that medicine has made you deaf. Now don't talk so loud," I said. "Everyone can hear you."

She continued anyway.

"Did you notice Claire has already taken three potted plants from the casket and placed them by the back door. She told me, not asked mind you, but told me, she was taking them home."

Lynne hissed at Mom to no avail. Mom waved at Claire and went on.

"She can have her three-dollars-and-ninety-five cent planter from Wal-Mart for all I care. You know it cost them fifty thousand dollars to join that country club, and all she brings is that three-ninety-five planter."

My mom has a tendency to exaggerate, so no one questioned a membership fee of fifty thousand for a country club in Wakarusa, Indiana. Besides she'd never admit she was wrong. Mom finished her dissertation on the three-ninety-five planter just as Claire joined us.

"Lovely planter Claire," Mom said.

"Girls," Claire said and took Lynne and my hands. "Girls. Girls. Girls. It's been so long. The last time I saw you, RaeAnn, I think you were just learning to ride a bike."

I rolled my eyes. I'd seen Claire last Easter and the Easter before that. Both times she'd said the same thing. I would have liked to think she was senile, but I knew better.

"And now you're getting married," she said. "How...," she paused, searching not for the right word but for the wedding gift she'd send. A check for five dollars? Dish towels? No, she decided. A set of marble coasters. She'd won them at the church bazaar and already had plenty of coasters. "...delightful," she finished. "Have you met the preacher? Oh, Sammy, Reverend Sammy."

Sammy, who has those kinds of eyes you can never be sure what or whom the person is looking at, was searching the room, head bobbing like a dog in the rear-view window. Claire barked, "Here, Sammy." And Sammy headed our way.

"Very pleased, very delighted, very happy to meet you," Sammy gushed.

I stared at his right eye, then his left, then his right, and then finally I crossed my eyes at him. He continued to pat my hand and nod his head. With one eye fixed on heaven and one fixed on hell, I was sure he couldn't see me. In fact, I followed the line of vision of his left eye and saw that it was focused right on Ida Mulcrackin's crotch. Someone had forgotten to point Ida's orthopedic shoes inward when they sat her down. Her legs were as far apart as Sammy's eyes.

"You must be RaeAnn," Sammy said. "I hear you're getting married."

I looked at Mom. She raised her eyebrows as if to say "How should I know." I looked at Daddy. He was blowing air through his mustache. I looked at Lynne. She tilted her head toward Tilly. Tilly was sitting in a chair talking to Celina's fat daughter. She smiled at us all and gave a little piano wave with her fingers.

And that's when the Marriage Trifecta was set into motion.

Chapter 2

The Old Maid and Other Wives' Tales

The marriage push wouldn't have been such a big deal, but my family had always had this incredible influence over me. We were a family of women: there was Tilly, my grandmother and head of the family; my mom Darla and her sister Aunt Kay; my sister Lynne and I; and Lynne's two girls.

Paw Paw, Tilly's husband, was the original man in our family of women. Then my dad, Ray, somehow wormed his way into the heart of the family, and we considered him a key member, but everyone else was an outsider. We were clannish in that way—partly because there were so few of us and partly because of the way we were raised.

We were all raised the same. Tilly raised her two girls, Mom and Aunt Kay the same, and Mom in turn raised her two girls my sister Lynne and me in the same way. Lynne, in turn, was raising her two girls the same.

When I was little and used to cry, my mom would send me to my room. I'd storm up there, just wailing. She'd stick her head in the stairwell and scream, "Cry harder. I can't hear you." I'd cry harder. She'd scream, "I still can't hear you. You must not really be crying. Cry harder." I'd scream my head off. "Nope, I still can't hear you," she'd say. Finally I'd wear myself out. Tilly had done the same thing to her.

We also heard a lot of the "do you want something terrible to happen to you?" routine, documented with real life examples from our own neighborhood.

"Don't run through the house with that sucker. Do you want to poke a hole through your windpipe? Maxine Gregory was running through her house with a Dum-Dum and she tripped on a rug and poked a hole right through her wind pipe.

At that age, I didn't even know what a wind pipe was, but I never ran with a sucker after that.

"You better look both ways before you cross the street or

you'll end up like Billy, the cripple. He used to live across the street, and once he didn't look, and now he's a cripple."

"Do you remember Billy?" I asked Lynne.

"No, but he's a cripple now," she said.

Once when I popped a blister, she loaded me in the car and drove me by Eddie Schickenjanski's house.

"See this house here," she pointed. "Eddie Schickenjanski used to live there. He picked his blister, and he died."

"Who's Eddie Schickenjanski?" I said.

My mom paused, unsure.

"Eddie Schickenjanski is the boy that died from picking his blister," she said. When she was little, Paw Paw drove her by the house and told her the tale of Eddie Schickenjanski and that was all I needed to know.

Both Mom and Tilly were cautious mothers, worried that something would happen to their precious children, so we were constantly reminded of what *could* happen. Ordinary appliances became fearsome items that could maim, even kill, if we weren't careful.

"Remember Andy Smitty's son. You know from the Legion. He was making some toast, stuck a fork in the toaster and kaplooey. He's dead," mom told me.

"Sally Firkin doesn't have all her fingers. She stuck her hand in a blender."

"Jeff Pilgrim had to have his foot amputated after he got it stuck in the lawn mower. They looked all over the backyard for his toe."

Our neighborhood was full of amputees, cripples, and ghosts of headless children that did not listen to their mother when she said not to hang their head out the car window.

"Your head's going to come flying off. Then you'll be sorry."

Tilly had also passed on these absolute truths that my mom used on us. They both had a way of convincing us that what they uttered was totally and indisputably true. When my mom said bread crusts would make my hair curly, I ate my bread crusts. So when my mom and Tilly said that Aunt Kay didn't get her 38 double D boobs until she was 17, I patiently waited until I was 17. "Maybe it was when she was 18," they said. Then I was 18. "I think she was 19," they said. Why I even wanted curly hair and big boobs was beyond me. Probably because they lead me to believe I *should* have curly hair and big boobs. "Aunt Kay was flat as a board until she was 17," they'd said. "Look at her now."

Tilly told me that the birds when they sang "purty-purty" were actually calling "pretty girl" to me. She acted as if I were the most beautiful, gifted child in the universe. And I guess I believed it without looking too closely in the mirror.

And then one day I caught a glance of myself sideways, as I really looked to others, and I realized they'd been lying to me all along. I mean I wasn't hideous or even plain, but I definitely wasn't beautiful. I had a ski-slope nose, short teeth, no chin, and a flat ass. All of us, in fact, have flat asses and flat heads. My Aunt Kay claimed that it was because Tilly let her lay in the crib too much, but that wouldn't account for Lynne and my flat heads. It was another family trait—another thing that bonded us all together. The flatheads.

They said I was a beautiful baby, the prettiest baby to be delivered at that hospital. And I believed them. I had seen one picture of me—I am a second child, so there were approximately 4 pictures of me as a child—and I was fat. I guess that made me cute. I mean I wasn't wrinkly or red or fragile. I was like a big baby doll—a child you could tote on your hips, toss in the air, tickle until I was blue in the face.

In eighth grade, I was 5'8" and weighed right around 100 pounds. They said I should be a model, and I believed them. I was like a tree, though, I shot up lengthwise quickly, and then my trunk and limbs filled out.

Everything fit with my body—except that my body was off center. I had scoliosis of the spine which means that my backbone was shaped like an "S." My hip bones and shoulder blades were uneven. That gives me the appearance of half my body arriving earlier than the other half, of hunching one shoulder all the time, of being 5'10" on my left side and 5'11" on my right side. I fancied my skewed body gave me a better perspective on life, I thought I saw things differently. And I fancied that the two years in the Milwaukee brace both saved and ruined my life.

At the peak of adolescence, I was strapped in a Milwaukee brace to correct my wandering spine. The brace was a huge contraption of steel, a human stretching and kneading machine. One thick steel bar, connected to the form-fitting body cast around my stomach and hips, jutted out and up across my body up to my chin. I couldn't drop my chin an inch in the front. And in the back, two thinner steel bars, similar to a headrest in a car, jutted from the back of the cast to the back of my neck. I had only limited movement of my head, and I looked like I was constantly scanning the sky for some sign from my Maker.

In addition to this, plastic pads were placed strategically and strung from bar to bar to shove my back into place where it was wayward. I was pushed and pinched from every angle twenty four hours a day for two years, except for baths.

I moved like a cement truck through my last years of grade school. It was hideous and uncomfortable. People stared at me and asked if I had been in an accident. I hated everyone that even accidentally looked at me. At a time when girls discover boys and were beginning to think about dating, I sat against the playground wall like an immovable piece of farm equipment and read.

It ruined my chances of going to the eighth grade dance, actually of going to a dance at all because I never developed that flirtatious, ask-me-out, worldly attitude of girls that had been asked on a hayride and learned the nuances of dating. Instead, I became friends with most of the guys I knew, and therefore, dating was not the most important thing to me throughout my life. In that way, my Milwaukee brace saved me.

Perhaps that was what started the marriage push. Was my family worried I'd be an old maid, a game we played endlessly? Had they caught a glimpse of me in the mirror, as I had, and seen that I wasn't as beautiful as they'd imagined? Were they afraid they'd never get rid of me—that I'd live at home with my mom and dad and Tilly forever? I rattled my brain thinking of any marriage advice.

Our upbringing was full of superstitions misremembered and

often spoke. I knew that if two people made a bed one was sure to get pregnant, that if I put my shoes on the bed I'd have bad luck and that if I put my nightgown on backwards I should leave it that way. When two people walked around obstacle on opposite sides, they'd better say "bread and butter" or an argument would soon follow. A bird in the house means a death in the family. If your palm itched, money was coming. If it was your nose that itched, it was company. I'm not sure what the itchings of other body parts portended.

All kinds of odd rules and rhymes whistled through my head, one for every occasion. "Find a penny pick it up, you will always have good luck." "Sing before breakfast, cry before supper." "Rain before seven, sun after eleven."

And the one thing I couldn't shake from my head is that deaths happened in threes.

It was Christmas, and every Christmas at our house was the same. The season starts with the annual tree decorating ceremony. Two years ago our Christmas tree fell on Tilly. The year before that it couldn't fall because in my dad's attempt to fit the tree in the stand he sawed too much of it off, and he had to wire the tree to the window. That year the tree was straight and actually stood up. We were putting the lights on.

"Ray, you didn't do a very good job at hiding the lights. I hate when you can see all the wires," my mom said.

My sister, who had made a special trip over for the ceremony, held up a piece of Styrofoam with felt and a trace of glitter Elmer-glued on it.

"We are not putting this pathetic piece of shit up are we?" she said. "Let's not put the homemade ornaments on."

I stood aghast.

"I made that pathetic piece of shit, and yes, we're putting on all this stuff," I said holding up a box of remnants of grade school art class. "Besides I see you've already tenderly placed that construction paper bell with that dumb Christmas poem in it on the tree."

"That poem won a prize in second grade."

"The homemade ones are my favorite," my mom said. She was putting on tinsel one strand at a time.

"I hate tinsel. Isn't this my year for no tinsel?" I said.

"Last year we didn't have tinsel. This year we have tinsel. Here put some on—one strand at a time."

I smiled at my mother and hurled a handful at the tree when she turned. Finally we were ready for the final ornament—the Star.

"Daddy, Daddy," we called, "come put the star on."

The star of our tree was a hand-painted, wooden Santa in a red and white Indiana University basketball uniform with my dad's old college number.

"Pretty soon, you'll have to look for your own star," Tilly said.

"What do you mean? Daddy will always be my star," I said not really getting her point.

She marked something down on a pad of paper, and I should have been more curious, but I was too busy watching Lynne sort through the homemade ornaments to find only hers.

I was glad Lynne was there. Christmas isn't the same without your sister, your only sister. She was pregnant again, and I liked just looking at her, imagining the new baby. She had said I could come in the delivery room with her, so I especially felt that this baby was mine, and I wanted time to study her over Christmas. Especially since I had a bad feeling since the funeral.

On Christmas morning, I played Santa and passed out the presents to everyone, reading the name tags aloud. "To Lynne. From Anheseur Busch. We appreciate the business," said a package that contained a Budweiser sweatshirt. "To Darla. From Smoky Bear," said a radar detector for my mom's Trans Am. She had just gotten the first speeding ticket of her life weeks ago. A nightgown to Tilly read "To Tilly. For our honeymoon. Love, Duke." Duke was one of Tilly's suitors.

We ripped through the packages opening a variety of perfume, jewelry, nightgowns, clothes, books, and more. During all this, my dad snapped pictures with his Instamatic camera. The pictures, like all the other pictures from Christmases gone by, would remain black and indistinguishable for Christmases to come. Ever since he picked up the camera from a garage sale a couple years ago, the only pictures that came out award-winning clear were thirteen pictures of me when I had all four wisdom teeth pulled, and my dad delighted in my swollen face. "She looks like a fat chipmunk," he said aiming the camera at me. Despite the fact that those were the only photos he has to show for all his camera work, he still snapped away every Christmas and waited for the pictures to develop, a tradition we had come to expect along with the passing of the mystery package and the missing presents.

A few years ago, my dad had ordered a diamond bracelet, ring, necklace and earrings for my mom for $19.95 from a late-night TV ad. Each year we passed the lovely diamond collection set back and forth among us. We all wondered who would get the mystery package this year.

Every year, there was at least one missing package. At their respective houses either my mom or my aunt screamed at their respective husbands, "There's a package missing." My dad or uncle would then rummage through their room while we eagerly hoped it was for us. It was usually something anticlimactic like underwear with reindeer on it or Post-a-note stationery. Once it was my ten-speed bike.

One year my aunt even went so far as to claim the missing presents had been stolen. She didn't even say "Merry Christmas" when we walked in. Instead, she greeted us with, "Some little brat stole some of the boys' Christmas presents. I'd like to get my hands on the little shit. It has to be someone we know."

The story went that some hoodlum broke into the house, knew the exact hiding spot of these select presents, found them, and stole them. Nothing else was taken. My aunt made a list of the stolen goods which she read to the police when they came: "One argyle sweater vest, size medium; one Indiana sweatshirt, red with white letters; a CD; and a portable TV." The police took the report, and we talked about the crime all day, offering suspects, figuring means of entry, and so on.

All the gifts were recovered that day. In the middle of going to the bathroom, my aunt claimed God spoke to her and said "suitcase." She came tumbling downstairs with her pants half up lugging a suitcase. All the gifts were inside, including the argyle sweater vest, size medium.

"I must have forgotten I hid them there," Aunt Kay said sheepishly.

That year the traditions came together. There *was* a missing package and it was for me. The tag read, "Next year it better be the real thing, Love Tilly." Inside was the diamond ensemble.

Chapter 3

Can't Keep a Good Woman Down

The next week Tilly was in the hospital. She was having trouble breathing, so her doctor admitted her to the hospital for testing. Doctors always made Tilly nervous. She planned what she wanted to tell them—kept a list safety-pinned to her lamp shade—but the minute she saw the doctor's white coat, her tongue rolled up and she began to cry.

"It makes me so damn mad," she said. "I feel like a big crybaby."

When the doctor came in to check Tilly, I explained some of the problems she had been having.

"Weight loss," I said. "She's shrinking away to nothing."

"How much does she weigh?" the doctor asked me.

"One hundred twenty," Tilly said. "I've been trying to lose a little weight for her wedding," she added, "but not this much."

"You are getting married?" the doctor said to me. Then he said. "How tall is she? "

"I used to be five-four," Tilly answered "but I'm so stooped now, I guess I'm about five-two."

"And what would you think someone five-two ought to weigh?" the doctor said to Tilly, the first time he had addressed her.

She shrugged.

"I'll admit," he said, "that thirty pounds is a lot of weight to lose. And a lot of extra weight to carry around." He turned to me. "She's by no means underweight. For her size and height, she weighs what she should. Perhaps before, she was a little overweight."

Tilly glared at him. "Don't talk about me like I'm not here," she said. "I'm not deaf, and I'm not senile. I'm not as old in my head as I look in my body. I have these bruises," she said and showed him her arms. "And I shake and I'm short of breath. And I go from doctor to doctor and they don't tell me a damn thing. 'You're old,' they say. 'What do you expect.' I suppose you'll tell me the same. Well, just you wait until you're old." She began to cry.

The doctor wrote a note ordering an EKG on a piece of paper and left without responding. I wheeled Tilly down the hall over to the lab for the test.

"Overweight, my ass," she said. "As if he's some spring chicken."

Once there, an attendant explained the test to Tilly.

"You'll have to ride that bike," he said. "And we'll take pictures of your heart."

"I don't know how to ride a bike," she said. "And I've got Parkinson's."

"We'll help you," he said. The attendant wheeled Tilly over to the bike and told her to climb on.

"How the hell am I supposed to get on the bike, you idiot. Fly? Jump? Jesus, if I could ride a bike do you think I'd be here?"

The attendant tried to help her lift her leg over the bike, but her shoe got caught on something, and she got stuck. I started to giggle. Tilly did, too. The attendant called another man over, and they decided to lift Tilly on the bike. She really started laughing then, and her body went limp. Her gown was flapping, and her eyes were watering as the two attendants held Tilly aloft over the bike. They banged her hip into the side of the bike.

"Be careful, that's my broken hip," she said.

They struggled and finally managed to perch her on the seat. They rearranged her a little.

"I feel like I'm sitting on two soup bones."

"Are you ready?" one said. "We're going to let go." They began to ease away, and Tilly leaned precariously to one side. They rushed back.

"No wonder you never learned how to ride a bike," Tilly said to me.

"I can ride a bike," I said indignantly.

"Huh. You should have seen her. Eight years old. Her dad would hold her on one side, and she'd lean. He'd move to the other and she'd lean that way. Her Paw Paw was going to get her one of those big three wheelers. She never did learn to ride. She just made her Dad jog her up and down the street on the bike 'Look, I'm riding,' she'd holler. We'd all laugh."

"I can ride a bike," I repeated.

"Now Tilly," one attendant said. "You're going to have to hang on." He lifted her dead weight arm and placed it on the handlebar. "Hang on."

"That's the arm I broke. It doesn't work. You know those damn doctors can never do anything right."

They tried for several minutes to balance Tilly on the bike, and finally decided to both hold her while running the EKG.

"Pedal," he said.

Tilly would pedal once around and her foot would slide off. One of the attendants would let go to put her foot back on the pedal, and she'd tilt over to one side.

"I'm falling you idiots. Do you want to break my other hip?"

They re-perched her and her foot missed the pedal. Finally, they claimed she was done.

"I hope you got your pictures," she said, "because I'm not coming back."

It turned out that Tilly had a bad heart valve, and the doctor recommended heart surgery.

"I can't guarantee it will help," he said "but we can try."

Lynne, Mom, Aunt Kay, and I debated the surgery. Tilly didn't do well in the hospital. One of her friends knocked her down during an icy spell, and Tilly broke her hip. During that stay in the hospital, the drugs they gave her made her hallucinate. She thought there was a revolving door in therapy and that my mom was scrubbing the halls in the hospital in the middle of the night. They changed her medicine, and we thought she was fine. Lynne called, and Tilly told her she had a new roommate.

"She wears diapers and plays with herself when a man comes in the room. It's disgusting. If I'm ever laid up in the hospital with diapers on playing with myself, come put a bullet in my head, okay? Promise me," she said. "I can't talk now. Some idiot in 6A set his mattress on fire, and they're moving us around."

"Let me talk to a nurse," Lynne said, fearing Tilly was again hallucinating.

"Tell my granddaughter I'm not nuts, Cracklin," Tilly said.

"This is Nurse Cracklin. The hospital is indeed on fire, and Tilly is fine. Her roommate has suffered a brain hemorrhage."

Tilly recovered from her hip, and then she broke her arm. She got up in the middle of the night to cut her hair and tripped on the rug. She had surgery to put a new shoulder in, and then later she had her toes fixed. She wrote me this note:

Dear Sweetie

Back to my roommate. Her back killed her. Therapy killed her. Pills weren't strong enough She could really get around good except when the doctor was in. I enjoy her, though. Her mother got her fourth man in a big wedding this Sunday. I came in with the worst hangover in all my 69 years. My roommate, Madge, was mad at her mom who had four bridesmaids and a long veil that Madge said he probably couldn't even lift up. TV coverage. Reception line, etc. Madge said after the wedding all they could probably do was sniff at each other. I cracked up.

I guess they thought Madge wasn't going to pull through because her relations were hanging around her saying, 'Madge, you know that settee you have? Can I have it?' One son-in-law wanted to buy her a really nice chair for her birthday. 'Why not,' he said, 'we'll be getting it back eventually.'

I came home feeling like I was walking backwards. But you can't keep a good woman down."

The surgery went fine, and we were relieved. I visited her every day.

"I look like Buster Brown," she said. She scrunched her face up, stuck her tongue out, and started to cry. he always stuck her tongue out when she was really mad or about to cry. I let her cry for awhile, until she finally stopped.

"I've been looking high and low for a doctor for you. This family could really use a doctor. I haven't spotted any yet. Or any for me either." Then she looked around the room. "Do you see the baseboards spinning around?"

"What?"

"The baseboards are spinning," she said and then added hopefully, "aren't they?"

I studied the motionless baseboards.

"And," she said, starting to cry again, "and I see a green bean hanging from that rod."

I wanted to laugh and I wanted to cry, so I laughed just a little.

"Tilly, you know there's not a green bean hanging from that rod."

"I know, but I *see* one! Last night I saw Kay standing on the end of the bed trying to steal that TV. And," she said, "she didn't have any clothes on."

The TV was suspended by a cable from the ceiling. I tried to picture my naked aunt holding the TV up. I didn't want to say anything because I'd really laugh, and I knew it wasn't funny, so I nodded.

"At first I thought it was the Statue of Liberty, but then I recognized her flat ass, so I started yelling. Ask my roommate."

"She did," her roommate said. "She wanted help, so I got up, and she threw her bedpan at me."

"I was aiming for the hall to get the nurse in here."

Her roommate went on. "I know how she feels. When I woke up I thought I was in a hotel in Bloomington. That's where George and I spent our honeymoon."

I smiled at her, and Tilly said, "Liza's in for a simple hand operation."

"My name is Elsie," her roommate said. "She keeps calling me Liza."

"*Liza* moans and groans over her little hand and keeps me awake," Tilly said in a loud voice.

I tried to smile a weak apology to Elsie, but she had gone back to reading her soap opera magazine.

"Is that a little dog sitting on my table? See his tail?"

I twitched the phone cord. "This is a phone."

Then I picked up the dog/phone and called my mom, who called the doctor, who switched her medication and ordered a beer for Tilly every night with dinner. When she started to feel better, she got back on the marriage routine.

"It's time you met someone," she said. "You better be on the lookout."

"How did Paw Paw and you meet?"

"I don't remember."

"Where did he take you on your first date?"

"I think we went and got a sundae."

"What kind did you get?"

"How am I supposed to know? Why do you care anyway?"

"I'm just curious."

"Curiosity killed the cat."

"Satisfaction brought him back," I said. "Did you know you wanted to marry him?"

"No, but he knew he wanted me. He always did the chasing. I didn't realize what a catch I had until he died. Or maybe it was when I was around fifty. You better look around, girl, and be thankful."

"How did he propose? On his knees?"

"Jeepers," she said, "I'm 72 years old. How the hell am I supposed to remember." And then she thought about it. "Well, I remember we had to hock his mother's wedding band to get a marriage license. Then I lived at home, and he lived at his house for about a year after we were married."

"You lived apart?"

"Had to. It was the Depression."

"What was Paw Paw like when you were first married?"

"Just like you. A shithead. Oh, and he was jealous as hell," she said as if she'd just remembered. "He didn't like for me to go out without him. He bragged that I couldn't go out in the car when he was at work. I told him I sure did and sure had been. He said I couldn't have because he'd been checking the mileage. I told him I unhooked it. He said I didn't know how, but I went out to the garage and showed him how to unhook it.

"I used to cat around with Aunt Esmerelda. She was dumber than hell, married to Petey, Paw Paw's brother the policeman. She never did have anything decent to wear so I said, 'Why don't you open a charge?' Of course, I had plenty of nice things to wear. So I took her up to Ayres, with Petey Junior in the buggy, and had her tell them she was a policeman's wife and arrange to get credit. Then she went and charged a fur coat. I convinced her to get it monogrammed so she wouldn't have to worry about taking it back." She laughed. "And Katie. Well Katie was always in trouble."

I had seen pictures of Tilly and her sister Katie in tight black skirts holding bottles of whiskey and playing cards. Once mom told me that Tilly was supposed to go to a shower, but instead went to Barringers Tavern. Mom went into the house side of the tavern and played paper dolls. When they left to go home, Paw Paw was lying in the back seat of the car.

"Shh...," he said. "I'm playing a trick on your mother."

I asked Tilly about the tavern story.

"Mom said that you left her in the car and all she had to eat was a jar of olives," I told Tilly.

"Your mom's full of shit."

I smiled.

"One time I did leave her in the house by herself," she said. "I saw a mouse in the closet, so I shut the door real quick, left your mom in the crib, ran out on the front porch, and sat there all day until someone came home." My dad was madder than hell.

"My dad asked me, 'What did you do with Darla? Leave her in the house by herself?' I said, 'She doesn't know better to be scared.'"

"Did your daddy like Paw Paw?" I said.

"Yes."

"Everyone liked Paw Paw," she said. "But most important of all, I loved him like there was no tomorrow."

Chapter 4

Horses Asses

"You'll meet someone tonight," Tilly said to me.

She was back from the hospital good as new, watching me get ready to go out. Tilly was optimistic, telling me that Christmas wasn't a good time to meet someone because they worried about buying you a gift or inviting you home to meet the family.

"It doesn't give them enough time," Tilly said. "But the New Year—that's a good time to start your hunt. In fact, tonight just might prove to be lucky."

"How do you know?" I said.

"It's in the stars. You're going to be getting engaged before next year. I'm sure of it."

Tilly bought horoscope booklets for everyone in the family and kept them in her bedside drawer with her dream interpretation book. She faithfully read everyone's horoscope and would frequently call, predicting good tidings or portending disasters.

"Don't ask Dr. Killenbrew for the day off," she advised Kay, long-distance. "Not a good day for favors."

"Don't buy that car today," she told my dad. "Be wary of promises made today."

I often wondered whether those books contained Tilly's little tidbits or whether she made them up to fit the occasion.

"You'll meet someone today who will have great impact on your life," Tilly read.

"If you say so."

"It's in the stars," Tilly called out the window as I left. "Smile a lot and be nice to everyone. You never know."

Sam and Trixie, my two best friends and I were going to the Bulldog. We'd been going there since we were 18, and I either knew everyone already or I didn't want to know them. Sam's, Trixie's and my childhood were the same. They only differed in the color of uniform we wore. Sam came to St. Jude's in fourth grade, and we wore blue plaid jumpers. Sam gained popularity (or I should say notoriety) quickly. She gave her enemies swirlies and was the best kickball player in the school's history, winning the CYO championship every year she played. She was the most confident, loudest person I knew. While the rest of us tiptoed across the ice to our cars in the winter, Sam ran and slide across the parking lot, waving her arms and talking loud. Her father was a judge and what passages of law she could not quote, she made up.

Sam married her grade school sweetheart right after high school. "He asked me to marry him in first grade. I said okay," she explained. "Then he called in his marker."

Trixie had attended Little Flower where she wore a green plaid skirt, won spelling bees, and sketched clothes designs in a little notebook. Fastidious about her appearance, Trixie had rich, red hair, flawless skin and big boobs. She never ceased to amaze me with her array of boyfriends and pocketbooks. That night she carried a purse that looked like it should house a pair of binoculars. She had just dumped her latest beau—a rich, Jewish banker.

"He brought me a sweatshirt from Acapulco," she said. "And get this. He tells me 'It was so expensive that I took the price tag off.'"

"What's the point?" I said.

"That's what I said. Besides, his mother was always hanging around his apartment, offering to change the sheets."

"And he smelled like corned beef all the time," I said.

"I caught Shreve's mom in our bedroom sniffing the last time they were over," Sam said.

"Really?"

"Well, I didn't actually hear any sniffing, but she was in there. She claimed she wanted to see our new dust ruffle."

"Yuck."

The three of us had situated ourselves at our table at the Bulldog. Eating popcorn and drinking Budweisers, we surveyed the landscape of the bar. Occasionally, we spotted someone worthwhile to flirt with.

"Tilly says I should get married," I said. "She's convinced I'll see someone tonight, someone I should marry. I have to be very alert so keep your eyes open."

"You want to get married?" Sam said.

"I want to be in love," I said.

"Love and marriage aren't even related," Sam said. "They aren't even kissing cousins."

"In love. I go out with some schmuck to some Italian restaurant and see all these lovey-dovey couples. I see some polyester woman with a whole pack of bobby pins in her hair and a huge inner tube rolling the world's largest bite of spaghetti around her fork..."

"See that's the point," Sam said. "There are more ugly people in the world, so there's more of a chance of them to pair up."

"Anyway this tub of lard is sitting with Mortimer the Meek, with his Sears Weather Beater white skin, and he's smiling at her like she's the only woman in the world. I want someone to look at me like that."

"A lot of guys have looked at you like that. And you've dumped them," Trixie said. "You say 'He gives me cow eyes.'"

"For instance?"

"Jack," Sam said.

"Graduation tassel still hanging from his rearview mirror. Walked like a wooden clothes pin. Danced like he had No Knocks gasoline in him."

"You are terrible," Sam said.

"I'm just quoting you," I said.

"Did I say those things? He did walk funny. Oh well, how about that football jock, Craig?"

"He was always punching me. Or slapping my leg like he was killing a fly. With him I'd have to survive with sex on my birthday and one other random holiday because he's more into ass-grabbing in the locker room. He said, and I quote 'Women are the potholes on the road of life.'"

"Ned," Trixie fired at me.

"Personality of a brick. I know I have the chatterbox syndrome, but when the goal of the evening is to get my date to utter five subject-verb sentences, the evening passes pretty slowly."

"Dave," Sam said.

"Personality of two bricks. Which means quantitatively he was better than Ned, but qualitatively worse. He said a little more, but it was less interesting."

"Mike."

"Couldn't get a word in edgewise. Tallied every beer I drank on a napkin."

"See. One's too quiet. One's too talkative. Mike was a pretty nice guy," Sam said.

"He called you an obnoxious drunk, remember?"

"That pompous ass," Sam said. "I never did like him."

"Since you're auctioning me off, how about the hot dog vendor downtown?" I said. "He asked my name the other day. So what if my betrothed sells weenies for a living."

"Frank," Sam said.

"Frank?" I said.

Frank was the one everyone loved and wanted me to marry. Frank worked at the gas station by our house when I was in high school. He went to a rival high school, another variation of the Catholic upbringing. He grew up on the East Side and was famous for several reasons: the cars he drove (a big blue van with only one seat and a fish painted on the side, a Cadillac with no muffler or trunk lid, and a Pontiac convertible that, if you wanted you could stop Fred-Flintstone style by sticking your feet through the rusted out bottom); the items he "acquired" (he once found a case of top hats); his fish stories; and his money-making ideas.

I met Frank through my dad. Frank was the only one who convinced my dad that he could indeed fix his `72 Ford Truck, which he inherited it from his dad, and that it would be a shame to get rid of such a fine piece of machinery.

"All it needs is a little tender loving care," he said.

My dad blew air through his mustache and invited him home for a beer.

The family immediately took to Frank. He offered to buy Tilly's car, a purple `64 Ford we called Erma, for one thousand bucks. "Of course, I don't have the money now, but I can tell you that car is a piece of art work. And I'm good for the cash." He asked Darla, my mom, for a date, and then said if he couldn't have her, he'd settle for her daughter.

Although, as Tilly said, "he was full of condensed horse shit," we all liked Frank. He had short reddish hair that he never combed, and he kept his Marlboro rolled up in his shirt sleeve like he was James Dean. He smelled like smoke because there was always a cigarette dangling from the corner of his mouth. His front tooth was brown from propping his cigarette up against it and smoking no-handed, as he pointed out the beautiful intricacies of my dad's truck engine.

Frank was currently living in Mexico, or so we thought. He usually came home for Christmas, but this year he disappointed me and didn't.

"Frank's undependable," Trixie said. "Matt."

"Matt," Sam echoed.

"Holy Toledo, I think we've got a winner. Call him over and see what he's doing July thirteenth."

Matt was indeed at the Bulldog. We all watched as he threw darts, swinging his ass to the left just like he did when he shot free throws. Matt threw a bulls eye, triple 20's and double 19's. Matt had perfect form at everything, even bowling. When he bowled, his right foot snaked in an arch behind his left as he threw a strike. He reminded me of bowler's I had seen on boring Saturday TV.

"What form," I said.

"What an ass," Sam said.

"Didn't we vote him nicest ass in high school?" Trixie said.

"Nicest legs," I said. "Jake Stepanovich had the nicest ass."

I guess you can say that Matt was my first love. I liked him as I grew up, and I had a big crush on him my senior year in high school. We were lab partners in Advanced Biology, and while he slit open the bellies of frogs, I studied his lips and imagined kissing him. He had sensuous lips—not too full, not too thin. One tooth, his snaggle tooth, pushed his upper lip out just enough to drive me wild. He always smelled clean, like toothpaste, soap, and deodorant. He wore red flannel shirts and gave me Hubba Bubba in exchange for my homework.

I was heartbroken when he invited Marian Himley, that cow, to the prom, and I purposely gave him the wrong answers to our final exam, that being the only clue that I was in love with him.

We had attended St. Jude's Catholic grade school together. I could picture his burr-hair cut bobbing on the altar during Mass, following Father around, making like a book stand to hold the big red tome filled with sacred Scripture, carefully placing the instruments of our religion on the white linen tablecloth over the altar. I could picture his red Chuck Taylor Converse sneakers peeking out from under his altar boy robe. "I'm going to heaven," he told me. "I'm an altar boy and that means I'm going to heaven."

Confident of his salvation, Matt jumped out of second-story window in third grade because Jeff Oldham dared him to. Landing like a cat, he turned and waved to our cheering class above. Sister Antoinette rapped him a good one for that.

I fell in love with this athletic grace in fifth grade when Matt was lobbing perfect quarterback passes to open-armed receivers. I drew pictures of our house, the house we'd buy when we married, and named our children Jake and Elwood, our dog Beauregard. At the swimming pool, Matt would catch me during sharks and minnows, a game we played. "Sharks and minnows," he'd scream in my ear holding me tightly above the water. "One, two, three." I was sure it was love.

But then sixth grade began. When Sister Marguerite would yell "Freeze," calling all of us to freeze in our exact position, Matt would perch on one foot, arms outstretched like a bird, tongue lolling out. He said he was a pterodactyl and made squawking noises, and I thought he was in idiot. Him and the rest of the sixth grade boys.

They made up a secret vocabulary, calling Cokes "Goggies" and milk "Lacha," and they pelted us with Milk Duds at the movies. In sixth grade, they stole all the band instruments from the high school, then gave them back hoping for a reward. In seventh grade, they slipped Kevin Connor's grandmother a sleeping pill and took her car out, driving past our houses, blowing the horn. In eighth grade, they hung out by the cafeteria walls during dances, shuffling their feet and laughing loudly. In ninth grade, they snuck into a storage room at the cinema, donned uniforms and walked home carrying cases of Raisinets. The next day, they proudly showed us the paper that reported their crime in the public record section. In tenth grade, they got their drivers licenses and started asking girls on dates.

We gazed at Matt for awhile until his girlfriend leaned into the picture and giggled into his ear. Matt.

"Three o'clock," Sam said. "At the bar. He looks like your type, RaeAnn."

All three of us stared at the bar. Sam's sighting was indeed my type; he was tall, dark and well, from our point of view, handsome.

"Call him over, so I can get a closer look," I said jokingly.

To my embarrassment, Sam wolf-whistled and waved at him. "Sorry, thought you were someone else," she said.

"He looks pretty cute to me," Trixie said.

"And Tilly said you'd met someone," Sam added.

We all turned and stared at him.

"Go over and talk to him," Trixie said. "See whether Tilly was right."

"I can never think of anything good to say," I said.

"The best first line I've heard is what Eric used on Emma. 'You have the most beautiful incisors.'"

"Speak of the devil," Sam pointed. "Earache and Enema."

And sure enough there they were, the couple of the decade, Eric and Emma. Sam and I had spent many years in both grade school and high school with Emma.

"She's been a hypochondriac since fourth grade. I was almost expelled for poking her with a pencil and giving her 'lead poisoning,'" Sam told us. "In fifth grade, she told us she had polio."

"Goodness," Trixie said. "Her neck is in a cervical collar."

"Her hearing's going," Sam said. "Didn't I tell you about that?"

Sam worked at a medical complex and knew the scoop on everyone's health because all the receptionists of all the various doctors ate lunch and compared patient notes.

"Do you know what the doctor said about her hearing?" Sam asked us.

"What happened to her neck?" Trixie said.

"The doctor said, and I quote `You could hear a pin drop in the next county.'" Sam was always quoting remarks she wasn't even in the near vicinity to even hear.

"What about her neck?" I said.

"Oh the neck injury is real. Only she can't gloat over it because the way it happened. I told you both that."

"No, you didn't."

"Tell, tell, tell," I said.

"Well, as best as we can reconstruct it, her and Earache were driving past Kelly's house. You know Enema hates Kelly because of Earache and Kelly and that time they were arrested for indecent exposure in Eric's pick-up truck. She had her top off and..."

"We know about that. Get on with her neck," I said.

"Well, Kelly was in the yard, and I guess Enema wanted to show how lovey-dovey they were, so she went to cuddle next to Eric in his car. Anyway, she lurched at him and jammed the car into park. Her head went flying into the dash, and she got whiplash or something. At least that's what I heard happened. I hope she doesn't come over her and give us her medical history."

"I hope she doesn't come over her and gloat about her wonderfully exciting, happy life," I said.

"Here she comes," Trixie said and nodded her head towards Emma.

"If she gushes and goos over what a wonderful guy, romantic man, conscientious lover, Adonis among mortal men Eric is, I'm going to tell her I saw him fucking his receptionist in his adjustable dentist's chair when I went in to get my teeth cleaned."

"I wonder how those two survive together," Trixie said.

"Are you kidding me?" Sam said. "Eric comes home, and they coo-coo for awhile, and then he says `Emma, Mrs. Gogerty had the biggest piece of gristle in between her second and third molar today....'"

"Shh...."

"Hello girls," Emma greeted us with a wave. She pointed her hand down and waved side to side with the back side of her hand, displaying her big engagement ring.

"Is that a mood ring?" Sam said.

"Did you get an invitation to Luellen's wedding? Why, everyone's getting married. Well, except you, RaeAnn."

"Hey, what about Maria Senawaltz?" I said.

"She's a nun," Sam, Emma and Trixie said in unison.

"Maybe someday," Emma said to me, teetering back to her table. She promptly sat on Eric's lap and started chewing on his neck like it was an ear of corn.

"Just the thought of going to her wedding makes me have a headache," I said.

"Here's something that will cheer you up," Trixie said. "Did you hear about the guy that broke his leg in some club in New York? When they took him to the hospital, they found he had a salami strapped to his leg."

"Seriously?" I said.

"His real one was probably the size of a cocktail weenie," Sam said. "He's got one the size of a cocktail weenie," Sam screamed and pointed towards Eric. He smiled and waved.

"Like Tilly says, there are more horses asses in the world than horses."

"That's right," Sam said. "So why do you want to get married to one? I'm going to tell Shreve I'm going out for a pack of cigarettes and never come back. When the kids ask, I'm going to tell them their dad joined the circus. Your dad's in the circus, honey. He's the world's biggest asshole."

"Sam," Trixie said.

"Excuse me," someone said over my shoulder. It was the guy from the bar. "Excuse me, but would you like to play darts."

And that's how I met Richard.

Chapter 5

No Keepsies

"He's in pantyhose," I told Tilly after I met Richard.
"Pantyhose?"
"Well, women's hosiery. His dad owns a big company in Chicago. He's based here in Indianapolis," I said. "I'm meeting him at his office tonight, then we're going to dinner."
"Can he get you a discount on hose?" Tilly said.
"I don't know. I'll check it out tonight."
The first thing I noticed about Richard's office was a huge map of his region with different color stick pins pinpointing the locations of the stores that carried his line. It took up an entire wall and looked pretty impressive. While he answered a call, I rearranged a few pins just to see whether the map was there, as I suspected, just for show. Then Richard showed me their computer system.
"I can make a pie chart of our anticipated sales by region, just like that," he said.
"Neat," I replied.
At dinner I discovered Richard knew a little something about everything. He talked the entire time.
"Do you prefer Southern or Northern Italian cooking? I just read a fascinating article in *Gourmet* magazine. The difference is basically in the seasoning of the sauce," he said.
"I prefer spaghetti and meatballs," I said.
"How about some calamari for starters," he said to the waitress.
Because it was our first date, I could hardly decline. Although I wasn't refined enough to know the difference between Southern and Northern Italian recipes, I did know that calamari was a fancy name for squid, and there wasn't a chance in hell that I was eating something as squeamish as squid.
"Try some," he said.
"I'll just save my appetite for my dinner."

"You must," he said and force fed me calamari.

I felt like I was at Schyler Barnhill's house and it was third grade. Her mother made me eat lima beans and drink milk. I tried swallowing the beans like pills, choked, and spewed food all over her new tablecloth. I wondered if Richard would invite me out again if calamari and red wine shot out of my mouth.

Despite the calamari incident, dinner went smoothly because Richard was an entertaining date. He had the gift of gab, but he also asked questions and solicited opinions throughout his oration. We talked, drank wine, and lingered over our dirty plates.

"Cappuccino?"

"No thanks."

"Surely you like cappuccino? It's delicious. I even have a cappuccino maker at my townhouse."

"Really, no thanks."

Richard ordered two cappuccino's, and I scalded my tongue trying to chug mine.

For our second date, Richard and I went to the art museum. I couldn't believe how handsome he was as I spied him out the dining room window. He wore brown wool pants, a rust-colored, crew-necked sweater, a tweed jacket with leather elbow patches, and loafers. Mom would have pirouetted with joy if she could have seen him, but the family was in Oldenburg, at Tilly's house, for the weekend.

During the car ride, Richard explained his love for modern art. He had taken an art appreciation class during college and fancied himself knowledgeable enough to give me a short history of the cubist movement. I, on the other hand, hated modern art and told him so.

"Oh, I'm sure you'll change your mind," he said confidently.

The first object we stopped to admire looked like a chunk of wood to me.

"I'm sure you can tell," Richard narrated, "this is the Madonna holding the Christ Child."

"Neat," I said. "Mother Mary on a slab of Formica."

He laughed and moved on to a bicycle tire chasing a man made of Popsicle sticks.

"The Machine Age overrunning man," he said.
"A kindergartner's art project."
"Now, RaeAnn."

I suffered through the museum. Richard only smiled and asked me when he was going to meet my family. I almost choked. I wasn't ashamed of Richard, he was gorgeous and presentable. And I wasn't ashamed of my family, but I was scared. What if he didn't like them? What if they didn't like him? Which was more important?

The first time Richard met the family, they were out in full force—even Lynne was there with her two kids and two of her Doberman pinschers, Sabrina and Max. Sabrina was in town to be mated, and Max just came along for the ride. I sat on the arm of the couch and pulled back the curtain to watch for him.

"Don't be so nervous. We're not the Muensters after all," mom said.

"Remember that time Daddy greeted Lou Stappas at the door in purple underwear?" Lynne said.

I look alarmed.

"Don't worry he's dressed," Tilly said. "I wish Dick would get here. I want to see him for myself."

"He goes by Richard," I said.

"I know what will take your mind off him," Tilly said. "Let's guess how many minutes until he gets here. Where's Ray? Tell him to get the stopwatch."

"I'll say 13," mom said.

"Mark me for 25," Lynne called.

"Wait. What are the rules?"

"Never mind. He's here."

I spied Richard out the dining room window. He eyed himself in the rear view mirror of his BMW before he got out and headed for the door. I felt like I should have waited in the tree out front, so when he drove by, I could jump down, land on the hood, and take off. I felt like running down the driveway and making a fast getaway, but it was too late. I heard him knock on the door and turned the corner in time to see Sabrina jumping on his cashmere sweater.

"Lynne," my mom yelled. "Come here and get your goddamn dogs."

"You'll have to excuse Sabrina," Tilly said. "She's pretty excited. She's in town to 'get a little,'" she said with a wink.

"I don't know why she brings the damn dogs every time," my mom said. "At least she left her husband at home." Mom eyed Richard and said, "I'm starting a new service—rent-a-son-in-law. Unhappy mother-in-laws can rent a son-in-law of their choosing. What do you think?"

Richard looked at me for help.

"Mom, Tilly. This is Richard. Where's Daddy?" I said.

Daddy came in from the backyard.

"Hey," he said to Richard, "can you give me a hand?"

"What's the problem now?" Mom said.

My dad blew air through his mustache. "I got the lawn mower caught on the strawberry barrel."

Our yard in now way required a riding lawn mower. In fact, it was probably even harder to mow with it, maneuvering around the obstacles, backing up, revving forward, backing up, revving forward. It was just the start of spring, and the grass didn't even need to be mowed. But my dad couldn't wait to get out that riding lawn mower. He had started moving things home from Grandma's farm.

"How in the hell did you get the lawn mower hooked on the strawberry barrel?"

"He can't help you, Ray," Tilly said. "He's all duded up. They're going out for Italian at Iarria's."

"I told you not to be using that damn mower."

Mom turned to Richard and said, "He doesn't know how to drive it."

"Maybe I could help," Richard said.

"Never mind." Daddy sighed. "I'll manage."

He turned and opened the back door. We could hear the lawn mower roaring in the backyard.

"He'll probably cut his foot off," Mom said.

"Are you any good at fixing things?" Tilly asked Richard.

He didn't have time to reply because Lynne descended the

stairs. Like a queen, she extended her hand.

"I'm Lynne," she said. "You must be Richard. Do you want to buy a champion Doberman?"

"Your dad's out back getting his foot amputated," mom said.

"The stud we're mating Sabrina with is one of the best in the state," Lynne said.

"Five hundred bucks for a piece of ass," Tilly said. "Imagine that."

"I have a cat," Richard said.

"Yuck." Mom stuck out her tongue at me.

As we left, I saw Daddy standing in the yard trying to cut down some weeds with one of my mom's big kitchen knifes.

"It's a machete," he said to me and waved.

Somehow I managed to get Richard out of the house and to Iarria's, my favorite Italian restaurant. Our family had been going to Iarria's since Tilly and Paw Paw were a young couple. Founded in 1934, the restaurant had those caricature statues of celebrities—Jimmy Durante and Marilyn Monroe and Louie Armstrong—on a shelf around the room and the best manicotti, the best minestrone soup, and the best atmosphere. The floor was red and white tiles, and the tables were steel with red and green tops, the benches were covered with red vinyl, the kind you might see in a diner. Next door, they had duck pin bowling.

Richard looked around when we got there, and I could see he was scowling. He opened the menu and studied it.

"They don't have seafood linguine," he said.

"I don't like seafood linguine."

"Milano Inn has seafood linguine."

"Milano Inn has lousy service, gross spaghetti, and rude waiters. It's overrated," I said. "I hate Milano Inn."

"I love their seafood linguine."

"Why don't you try the veal parmesan. It's delicious," I said.

I studied Richard across the table. He had on a pink cashmere sweater over a pink and white striped oxford shirt. Some guys would look like a flaming pansy in pink. On Richard, it only enhanced his dark curved eyebrows, green bedroom eyes, and smooth, tan skin.

Richard ordered lasagna, I got manicotti, and we sat in

silence until Sal brought our soup. Richard took a spoonful and didn't say anything. He ate his salad, and the garlic bread, and the lasagna without once saying he did or didn't like it.

Finally, he said, "Your family seems nice. I liked them."

I nodded. I wasn't that worried about him liking them, I was more concerned about whether they liked him. My family could make or break a relationship, easy, like snapping a pencil in half.

My family always had their fingers in my love pie. Fixing this one up, ruining that one. When I was seven we went to Virginia Beach, and they tried to pawn me off on some fat kid. My mom spotted him and thought it would be nice if I played with him. This nice boy had a burr hair cut and looked like a Weeble. Weebles wobble, but they don't fall down. Mom dubbed him Sluggo and invited him to our hotel room to play. When he knocked on the door, I hid under the bed, but my sister grabbed my ankles and pulled me out.

Sluggo had just been to Williamsburg and had a bag full of marbles. He said he'd teach me how to play, but we were playing for "no keepsies," meaning that if I won and knocked the marbles out of the circle I couldn't keep them. As I slaughtered him at marbles, all Sluggo could say was "Remember, no keepsies. No keepsies." When I reported back to mom about my marble date, at age seven, she got the biggest kick out of that phrase "no keepsies," that she repeated "Sluggo" and "no keepsies" throughout the remainder of my life. Every now and then she'd say "no keepsies" and laugh.

Sluggo wasn't my first love, a neighbor kid was. And looking back, I could see my mother's fingers in that little affair of the heart. Her and my "Heaven's" mother were friends. His name was actually Evan, but I called him Heaven and he called me Sweetie. We used to tie dish towels around our necks and run up and down the street, me Robin to his Batman. Our mothers stood in the driveway and talked about how cute we were.

My mom also tried to set me up with this grocery stock boy/deli boy when I was a teenager because he gave her a good deal on roast beef. She used to say if there was ever a war, and they had to ration meat, it'd be good to have a butcher in the family.

Tilly didn't like him because she bought a sandwich and showed it to me. On the inside where the bun was cut, the meat was thick, and it looked like one hell of a sandwich. A quarter of an inch past the cut, though, the meat dwindled out, and only the bites in the center were any good.

"See," she said, "they go to deli school to learn to stack it like that."

Mom wasn't the only one setting up love affairs for me. My sister and I swam competitively, and she liked to set me up with the little brothers of the big brothers on the team that she happened to like. One gave me a black eye. One did cartwheels down the hall of the hotel where we stayed at an out-of-town swim meet. He swam for a team in South Bend and used to write me letters about his golf game and his swim practice. I don't know what else I expected out of a love letter at nine, but "My fourth grade teacher is Mrs. Roberts. She is nice," didn't exactly make the grade. I can imagine my letters back were equally thrilling.

I had seen what Lynne had to go through with her boyfriends, so I was well prepared for the family tactics for getting rid of someone they deemed unworthy. The worst was "Private Eye." My mom hated that particular boyfriend, and somehow (this part is unclear) she claimed he had only one testicle. How she was privy to such information we were not sure. She called him "Private Eye," though, and she teased my sister about it incessantly. She would make me, a pawn in her chess game of love against my sister, parade around the living room wearing my great grandfather's monocle.

"Well, just ask him if you don't believe me," my mom said. "Or better yet, next time he comes over I'll ask him, and we'll get this thing squared away."

"Mother!"

Another boyfriend that Mom hated was dubbed "Weenie Arms" because he always talked about building up his physique and lifting weights.

"RaeAnn's bigger than him," mom said. "Hell, we could both knock the little bastard silly. He's a wimp—a weenie."

Mom again used me to prove to Lynne how ridiculous "Weenie" was. As a soldier in her army, I was instructed to stand behind him so that Lynne could see me. I was supposed to flex my muscles and pose like a body builder. Once he caught me and said, "I bet you're big enough to beat off a bear with a switch stick." Another phrase, like "no keepsies," much to my chagrin that has been repeated throughout my life.

One boyfriend we all liked was Lou Stappas. At thirteen, I used to look forward to Lynne's dates more than she did. I'd wear a special outfit just to answer the door, but once my dad beat me to it. On his way up from the shower—the shower was in the basement which was another story entirely—he greeted Lou at the door in bright purple jockey shorts.

"If you've scared him off, I'll kill you," mom said.

Lou Stappas was an architect in Philadelphia, and my mom mentioned his name every chance she got. Just like she reminded us she could have married Bill Whitaker, largest dog-casket maker in the Midwest. Lou sent our family a Christmas card every year, and once called my mom long distance from a job in California to ask about Lynne. Lynne, of course, was married, and as my mom grudgingly admitted, happily married to her pharmacist, Harry.

I figured it was best to find out the family's reaction to Richard before I committed myself. We were at Lynne's house. I sat at the kitchen table watching Lynne cook scrambled eggs. She was starting to show, and I couldn't wait for the next baby to arrive.

"I have to fix Hercules some scrambled eggs. The show is coming up, and eggs make his coat shiny," she said. Hercules was another one of their Dobermans. I figured Lynne was distracted enough with her dogs that I could bring up Richard without her making a big deal of it.

"What do you think of Richard?" I said. "Think I should marry him?"

"The nationals this year are in Louisiana. Won't that be something? We'll probably only show Hercules since Max still has trouble with his ear."

"You know I dreamt last night that you gave me a green monster with spikes on it for my birthday. It was as big as a twin bed and ate katydids. Tilly said it's a sign that I am envious of you and what you have."

"Hasn't Max gotten big?"

"Do you listen to me? Ever? All you ever talk about is those damn dogs," I said. "The poor girls. They'll grow up thinking they are dogs."

"What? What are you talking about? Did I tell you that Ciara was pregnant? She miscarried, we think, because we found a puppy head in the kennel."

"Lynne!"

"What?"

"Are you listening?"

"Yes, what's on your mind besides some dumb dream?"

"I tell you why I have nightmares. It's that coffin you make me sleep in. And those dogs yelping."

The log home that Lynne lived in was gorgeous, but small. When I stayed the night, I slept in the loft with the roof slanting directly over my head. It was like sleeping in an open coffin. The loft overlooks the living room, and Tilly slept there in a fold-out bed. With the dogs barking, the dryer running, Nadine crying, and Tilly snoring, I barely got one wink of sleep. In the middle of the night, one of the dogs shit on the floor. When Tilly got up to go to the bathroom, some squished between her toes. She gagged and snored and cussed the rest of the night.

"Did you know your youngest daughter is crawling around in a dog cage right now eating a dog biscuit?"

"That's okay."

"Pardon me?"

"The ingredients of a milk bone and a teething biscuit are basically the same. A teething biscuit breaks up and is easier to choke on, though."

"I suppose the milk bone is more flavorful, too," I said scooping, Nadine off the floor and yanking the biscuit out of her mouth. "This is dog food, Nadine. You are not a dog. Understand? When you grow up, I'm going to tell you how your mom let you eat dog food."

I handed her a glass of Hawaiian punch, and she started lapping it with her tongue.

"Look, she's drinking like a dog."

Lynne ignored me and set a plate of hotdog and ketchup in front of her daughter.

"Whatever happened to Frank," she said. "I liked Frank."

"Matt has a girlfriend."

"Frank, I said Frank."

I wasn't listening because I was watching my niece put her face on her plate and chew a piece of hotdog.

"Now she's eating like a dog," I said.

"All kids that age eat like that."

"She thinks she's a dog."

"Caroline did too," Lynne said. "Who's got the most money?"

I looked at her, puzzled.

"What have I been telling you all these years—marry for money."

"Tilly says you can't marry for money or sex because they both run out," I said.

"Marry someone with money," she repeated. "Personally, I think you should wait until you are at least thirty-five. You know have some fun."

"Thirty-five is too old. At thirty-five, you get that desperate look—even if you're not. I mean you can insist all you want that you're happy being single, and you might very well be. But other people start thinking of you as an old maid, and you start getting that old maid scent whether you want it or not. Besides I want kids. What are you planning on doing? Giving me a couple dogs to pretend they're my kids?"

"No, you can borrow my real kids any time you want. The last time you took them, you swore you were getting your tubes tied."

"You said the baby slept until eight o'clock, and she was up at five. And she shit on everything in the house," I said. "Still I would take them in a heartbeat." I smiled at Nadine.

"That's how it is with a baby. I tried to tell you. It's not exciting being married. Do you know what I did on my birthday this year? I went to Wal-Mart. Nadine got some bubbles, Caroline got a book, and I got a fly swatter and a new nozzle for the hose. We ate at McDonald's. That's marriage—manwiches, Nickelodeon, and a mini-van." But she smiled when she said it.

Lynne seemed to have a perfect life, two homes, a custom van, a motor home, two beautiful girls, and another one on the way. She was working on getting a boat—much to the delight of Tilly. She had a petite, perfect figure, green eyes with long eyelashes, and a husband who was constantly involved in money-making schemes. One year he made a killing on seaweed, and then he started breeding champion Dobermans, this in addition to his regular job as a pharmacist. All that for someone who used to sleep with two curls scotch-taped to each of her cheeks.

I stared at Lynne and smiled. She smiled back, probably already knowing what I was thinking. I picked up a brush and began to comb my hair.

"Ouch! Where'd you get this brush?"

"It's mine. It's good for the scalp. I had to look all over for one like it."

"Where'd you get it?"

"The pet store."

I dropped the brush and started scratching my head. "Hey. Daddy got a new camera. From another garage sale. Only twenty-five dollars."

"Do the pictures come out black?"

"No, amazing enough they don't," I said, and she looked surprised. "They come out all white. And he's raising fishing bait in the basement. I tripped over a carton of live crickets down there," I said.

"What brought this up?" she asked.

"You did," I said. "You remind me of Daddy sometimes."

Tilly came out of the bathroom. She had her new nightcap on. The new one made it look like someone had plopped a packet of wedding rice on her head. She started to make the bed.

"Richard didn't like Iarria's," she told Lynne. She said it as if it were God Richard didn't like. "Two make a bed. One gets pregnant."

"What's your cap on for?" I said.

"Shut up," she said. "You had to ask me last night if my head itched, and I got to thinking about all those dogs and couldn't quit scratching. I itched my hair-do out of place. It's not easy keeping myself up. You better hurry and get married while I still look half-way decent. Before I embarrass you."

"I guess when you fell in the bathroom at Lynne's wedding you didn't embarrass her."

"Hell, no. I was in my prime then." Tilly said.

"So what's the consensus then?" I said.

"On what?" Lynne said, which was answer enough.

Tilly waved her hand side to side as if to say "so so."

Chapter 6

The Happiest Man Alive

After the meeting-the-family episode, I didn't hear from Richard all week. I waited and waited, eyeing the telephone. Finally, the phone rang. I thought it was for me.

"Tilly, it's for you," mom said with a gleam in her eye.

I looked at her quizzically.

"It's Duke," mom whispered.

Duke knew Tilly before she married Paw Paw. He claimed Paw Paw stole her away, and he called her exactly one month after his own wife, Florence, died. He asked her out, and she said she better "face the music" and went. He drove her around in his pick-up truck to all his relations. "I felt like a horse," she said. "I felt like saying, `Yes, these are my own teeth.'" Although she avoided him and made up lies when he called, he occasionally caught her at home.

I grinned and Tilly grimaced.

"Hello," Tilly said in a fake voice. Then she waved me over and let me listen in.

"How are things with Margie?" Tilly asked right away. Margie was Duke's other 'girlfriend'.

"She's fine. We went on a vacation to a trailer park in the Ozarks and met the nicest people. I want you to know though, Tilly, we're not going steady or anything. Why if you gave me half a wink, I'd take you on vacation. Anywhere you wanted to go."

Tilly put her hand over her mouth and said, "As if I'd want to go to a damn trailer park."

"Hmmm," Tilly said, making no comment. "How has your health been?" she said into the phone. Then she said to me "Just listen. You'll see."

"Well, to be honest, Tilly, the last time I saw you I wasn't feeling too great. I was taking eight or ten pills a day, but I just wasn't feeling all that good. I didn't want to say anything to spoil our date because I don't like to complain. But I finally went to the doctor. I thought it might be a spot of pleurisy under my left lung. I wasn't sure what it was, but the doctor ran a bunch of tests and finally told me to quit talking all my medication. Except for what I take for my emphysema and high blood pressure. You know I have both."

Tilly held the phone away from her ear and rolled her eyes. We listened in some more.

"Well, I couldn't let him take those pills away. Why that was what kept me going, I thought. So I told him that I couldn't do that, but he said to try it, and I did. And by God a couple days later I felt better than ever. I take only two pills a day now, and I'm a new man. How have you been? Now let me tell you. Twenty-two years ago I got sick and had to go into the hospital. I didn't think I was going to make it. Right then and there I swore to the Lord if he helped me through this I wouldn't do a thing to hurt my health again. And I did get better. And since then I haven't touched a drop of liquor or a cigarette yet. Been twenty-two years. And I used to smoke two packs a day, and I'd come home and have a beer or two or three. I figured I deserved it. I worked hard, I brought home money, I was good to my family. If I wanted a drink, I was going to have it. But then I got sick and swore off the stuff, and I haven't touched it. Not a drop or a puff. You don't smoke, now do you Tilly? And I know you like your beer, but I bet you don't drink much, huh?" Duke finally paused.

"Just one or two," Tilly said and paused. "Just one or two *six packs.*"

"Pardon me?"

"Listen Duke," Tilly said. "I have to go. It's time for my medication." Tilly looked at me and mimicked tilting a beer can to her mouth. "Good-bye." She hung up without wanting for a response.

"See." Tilly said to us. "See."

"He seems nice," I said. "He'd take you places."

"Who wants to ride around to all the parks with him eyeing me, trying to hold my hand, and giving me a dissertation on his health every time I want to crack a beer. No way."

"At least you wouldn't have to worry about drunk driving. He might be a good match," mom said.

"You don't know shit from apple butter Darla," Tilly said. "Who needs the old fart anyway. He looks like an embalmed Porky Pig. We'd be like two mules in a harness. That's what marriage is–two mules in a harness."

"Wait," I said. "He tried to hold your hand? When?"

"Shithead. You're a shithead. I am going to bed."

Tilly went upstairs, Mom and I stayed in the living room, and my dad went to his workshop in the basement to continue work on his latest project. My dad was always busy with some craft project or another. The problem was he never finished them. He sent away for a Time-Life book describing how to put a bar in the basement. He got all the equipment he needed, he hammered the plywood into a bar-like structure, he super-glued the red counter top on, and he started installing the sink. The sink gave him some problems. It shot water all over the basement, so he quit work on the basement bar and turned to making picture frames.

He glued seashells and postcards with pictures of seashells to a piece of royal blue felt, made a frame for it, and hung it over the mantle.

"Get that ridiculous thing from over the mantle," mom said.

Lately he was working on his dollhouse. He bought a kit in Tennessee, a two-story Victorian home with a big porch, latticed windows, chimney, fireplace, the works. He planned to give it to my nieces for Christmas.

"Graduation," mom said. "He'll have it finished in time for the girls' college graduation."

He had done pretty well with this project. Not just content to assemble the house, Daddy wallpapered the walls, picking out a delicate pink floral pattern. He bought fake bricks and glued them on the fireplace; he shingled the roof; he installed tiny gold door hinges, door handles, and even a door lock; he carpeted the floors, selecting plush red carpet. Every night we'd be called down the basement. "Come here everybody and look," he'd yell. "I've put the trim on the porch."

We'd oooh and aaah. Meanwhile buckets of water were

leaking through our own roof, the fireplace hadn't been cleaned out since last Christmas, and the bathroom door was connected by the top hinge only.

The night before I visited him in his "workshop" and he was sitting with a needle and thread working laboriously.

"What's that?" I said.

"A quilt for the bed," he said and showed me a new kit he purchased to make doll furniture. "One hundred and four pieces."

To keep the wooden cut-outs of 104 pieces of doll furniture separate, he had collected and labeled little boxes. "Piece 4," one said. "Armoire."

"Looks nice," I said.

My dad smiled and blew air through his mustache.

Everyone loved my dad. You couldn't help but love him. Every month or so, he would exclaim, "I am the happiest man alive." And then he would give you a big bear hug. It was amazing he had turned out so well.

My dad was raised on a farm, and he was very close to his grandparents. In fact, they raised him.

"Gram gave me two rows at the farm," he told me. "I could grow whatever I wanted, and the money I made from what I grew, I got to keep. All summer long I worked. See, I wanted this beebee gun Uncle Neil had. I needed four dollars and fifty cents," he said. "At the end of the summer, I had about two fifty from selling the corn I grew. Neil gave me the gun, but he wouldn't take my money."

At the farm, the land, our land, expanded for as far as I could see. We even owned the land across the highway. Lynne and I would swing from a rope in the hayloft. We'd pick whatever we wanted out of the garden, a carrot, a strawberry, a mango, and eat it without even washing it. In the summer Grandpa turned on the irrigation, and Lynne and I ran wild in the mud.

Daddy was an only child, and he loved the farm. There were pictures of him atop the tractor, atop the fence to the garden, atop the hayloft. There were pictures of him chasing roosters, picking blueberries, climbing the apple tree. There was even a picture of him pissing on a cat.

My dad was a great athlete—cited by the state newspaper as the best high school basketball player, state-record holder in track. Although Jess wouldn't come see Daddy play in anything, she cut out every mention of his name. She also cut out the death notice of every relative, friend, friend of relatives. When we cleaned out the farm, we found drawers filled with obituary notices.

Jess wore bright red lipstick and kept my dad quiet as a child by turning on the vacuum cleaner. Afraid of the loud noise, he'd hide behind the couch when she turned it on. My grandfather was an engineer, had a basement full of gadgets, and refused to attend my father's college graduation. They raised my dad from the sidelines, reading about his triumphs in the paper, watching him from inside the house.

"You know what?" I said to my mom. She and I were sitting in the living room, waiting for Daddy to call us down the basement to admire his latest work. "I want to marry someone like Daddy."

"What did you just say?" my mother said. "Did I hear you right? I want you to go stand out in the backyard with grass up to your knees, two boats that don't work, a strawberry barrel that won't grow, a grill that won't cook, and a 1972 Ford truck that costs more in monthly repairs than car payments on a new one would be. Go stand out back and tell me again you want to marry someone like your father."

"So he isn't perfect, but he tries. He made you that lovely wall hanging," I said pointing to the felt thing with shells glued on.

"You like it so much I'll give it to you for a wedding present," she said.

"What was your wedding like?" I said.

"You know the story," mom said.

My mom and dad were married at the justice of the peace in Bloomington, Indiana. My mom wore a light blue suit and a hat. They were both sophomores in college. For a while they lived in converted army barracks. Then they moved to a trailer when my sister was born, nine months and six days after they were married. Five years and five miscarriages later, I was born. That same year, my mom had a hysterectomy.

I nodded and waited. I knew she would start the story.

"The minute your dad walked into my anatomy class I knew I wanted to marry him, so I accidentally took his notebook home from class." She smiled that certain smile she always did when she told me this story.

"You had it easy back then. In your era. People just put on their poodle skirts, fell in love, and got married. It wasn't so complicated."

"Easy? Ha. We lived in a trailer, ate peanut butter every night and saved bottle deposits to get a ninety-five-cent pizza on Friday. It wasn't easy little girl. We had to struggle."

"Tell me about when Lynne was born. What did Daddy do?"

"Oh, it was typical of your father. He was a wreck. I fixed him some soup, and he got out a can opener to eat it with. We didn't have a car, so he borrowed one. He came running out of the house with towels and a bottle of ink. The towels were for if my water broke, the ink for announcements. No pen, no announcements, just ink."

Both of their versions were the same. I wondered how many times they'd retold this particular story.

I laughed. "And when Daddy saw Lynne? What did he do then? She was an ugly baby, right?"

"No, she was a beautiful baby. She was just tiny. Ray could hold her in the palm of his hand. He just kept staring at her and looking at all that hair. Lynne's whole body was covered with hair."

"And me?"

"Oh, you were just like a little doll. Not pink or wrinkly like most babies. Why the doctor said you were the prettiest baby he'd ever delivered, and he was sixty-five at the time. The nurses fought over who got to take care of you. You were a beautiful baby."

I smiled proudly. This was my favorite part of the story.

"After you were born and I had the hysterectomy, I came

back from the recovery room. Your father was sitting in my room all wide-eyed," mom said. "He held my hand so tight, he cut off my circulation.

"'Do you want anything,' he asked.

"'No, Ray, I'm fine. I'm just tired,' I'd say and try to go to sleep.

"'Is there anything I can get you?' he'd ask again.

"'I'm fine,' I told him. Every time I'd close my eyes, he'd grip my hand.

"'What are you doing?'

"'Going to sleep.'

"Three minutes later he'd wake me up by clenching my hand. `Are you sure you're okay? Can I get you anything?'

"'Really, I'm okay.'

"Your dad stayed awake all night in that chair next to my bed. Just holding and squeezing my hand."

I smiled. If Lynne and I had anything wrong with us, a stubbed toe, a splinter, a loose tooth, we wanted Daddy. With his gentle hands, he'd reach in and pull loose teeth painlessly from our mouths, splinters from our fingers. He had his own special remedies when we were sick. For instance, if we had a sore throat, he'd bring home Popsicles and rainbow sherbet. If we had a cold, he'd make us hot toddies. Chicken soup and Sprite were served for the flu. He'd hang around outside our door asking, "Is she awake yet?"

"Let her sleep," mom would say.

The minute our eyes popped open, he'd be in with our plate or tray of goodies. No matter how terrible you felt, we always ate whatever he brought, for disappointing my dad was a sin none of us ever wanted to commit.

I smiled and said, "Someone like Daddy."

"Sure. Look at your dad. He walks in every night, asks `What's for supper?', gets a beer, sits in his chair and falls asleep balancing his beer can on his belly. Last night I woke up and he was standing over me with a lantern. A lantern! He said his teeth had flown out while he was snoring, and he was looking for them."

I pictured my father with his Coleman Lantern and his

jockey shorts with little Cupids, looking for his teeth.

"Did he find them?"

"Yes, they were snagged on the comforter."

"How are his new teeth doing?" I asked. Daddy had just gotten a new set of false teeth.

"As he put it, he can eat a dill pickle, so he thinks they're fine."

We both smiled.

"Let's look at the pictures," I said. I knew it wouldn't take too much convincing to have mom get out her box of treasures.

My mom kept a steel box of her mementos under her bed, and every now and then she got it out and fingered the clippings and pictures and dried flowers. One clipping showed my mom sitting on the grass at the Kentucky Derby with her white dress fanned out around her. She was sipping what I imagined to be a mint julep. The headline read, "This is a horse race not a beauty show." We had been through this box a million times. Each time she showed me something new.

We went up to her room, and Mom took out her beloved box. I sat patiently, waiting for her to show me what she wanted me to see this time.

"Here's a letter from your dad," she said and then she read parts of it to me. "Forgot to pick up my paycheck. But all I need is your love. I can live on your love alone."

I was surprised that my dad etched such a line.

Then she read further, "I've been constipated for 165 days."

That sounded more like my dad.

Daddy came upstairs.

"You didn't touch that heat did you, Ray?" mom said, back to practical matters.

Daddy blew air through his mustache.

"RaeAnn, go turn the heat back down."

My mom and dad waged a war over the heat. Mom would put it around fifty degrees and Daddy put it over seventy. I either woke up with the covers over my head afraid I'd freeze on they way to the bathroom or stuck to the sheets, depending on who went to bed last.

"I've got more goose bumps than a dill pickle factory," my

dad said. "Please leave the heat alone."

"Put on a sweater," mom said. "I was just telling RaeAnn about living in Bloomington." Back to the romance.

My dad smiled and then decided to join in the retelling, probably because he liked the story as much as my mom. Or he wanted to distract her from the heat issue.

"Jerry Thompson had the only car on the block," my dad said. "I had to borrow it to take your mom to the hospital when she had Lynne."

"You had to stick your foot out to stop car," mom added.

"We'd go to the gas station and get twenty-five cents worth of gas and a dollar and a quarter for brake fluid," my dad continued.

"We'd save our bottle deposits to get a pizza."

"Or trade in our spare tires. 'I gave my spare tire last week,' Jerry would say," Daddy added.

"All our neighbors in the trailer court were in the same boat. Poor like us."

"Except for the next door neighbor's. They'd grill big old steaks and drive us crazy. Here we didn't have enough money among us to get a pizza with cheese, no toppings, and they were grilling steaks."

"When we lived in the army barracks, we had cockroaches, mom said. "I called Tilly crying hysterically. I put cups of water around Lynne's crib so that if they climbed up they'd fall off and land in the water and drown."

"Your mom said 'I'm leaving.' And we got in the car and drove to Indianapolis that night."

"And remember Lynne climbed out of her crib in the trailer and fell. I thought your dad was going to have the big one then," mom said.

"I was painting the oven black one time, and I turned around and there was Lynne, looking like a little pick-a-ninny."

"We had a car when we lived in the army barracks. A fifty-seven Kelly green Cadillac," Daddy said. "I paid seven hundred and fifty dollars for it. I can see it now."

"And you promised to quit smoking if we got that Pontiac convertible. 'If I can just have a convertible, I'll give up smoking,' he promised me. I found the cigarettes under the front seat the second week we had the car."

"Your dad always got us the greatest deals on cars. On everything," Daddy said.

"Your dad," Mom said to me "was afraid they were hot because your Paw Paw got them from a *friend* on the Southside. He got us this Admiral TV, and it broke. When the repairman came to fix it, you should have seen how nervous your dad was. Pacing around, blowing air through the mustache, and worrying that the repairman would somehow know it was stolen. Your dad wanted to throw it in the canal."

"Was it stolen?" I said.

"RaeAnn." Mom frowned.

"Hey Daddy, how did you know Mom was the one?"

My dad blew air through his mustache a couple times.

"Hell, I don't know," he said.

"Come on Ray, you remember," my mom said.

"I'll tell you what I remember about your mom. She had the biggest set of boobs I'd ever laid eyes on. I saw those boobs, and then I looked up and saw her big brown eyes. I guess that's all she wrote."

"Ray!"

"I'm the happiest man alive," my dad said. And then he gave me a big bear hug that hurt.

My mom was looking at a picture from some formal dance at college. In the picture, my dad had on tux with short pants and knee socks and looked pretty goofy. My mom had on long gloves and a white chiffon dress. Her lipstick was red and just perfect. She smiled at the picture.

Chapter 7

Kowtowing

Richard called the next day and asked me to go on a ski trip.
"I don't ski," I said.
"I'll teach you."
I went along skeptically, but the whole thing turned out to be the first of several disasters. Richard knew *everything* about skiing, so he refused to allow me to take a lesson. I started on the bunny hill, got my ski pole caught on my boot trying to grab the tow rope, and fell. When I did get to the top, I let go too soon, and the beginners behind me fell like dominoes. I shyly inched away and started down the hill, calling for Richard to watch me. He watched as I zoomed at full speed down the bunny hill, into and over a 250-pound beginner. She was barely fazed. She pointed her ski pole at me and said something obscene. I couldn't hear her because my ears were ringing, and I wasn't sure I was breathing.

"Maybe I should take lessons," I said.
"No, you just need to learn how to snowplow. Turn your ankles inward, and dig your skis into the snow. Try it again."

I tried it again, made it down the hill safely, past Richard screaming "Snowplow," past the benches where you put on your skis, past the crowd of people in front of the lodge. I finally slowed enough to grab a tree to stop and looked back the 100 yards I had snowplowed.

"I have weak ankles," I yelled to Richard.
"Let's try a real hill," he said.
I should have clung to that tree by the lodge, but instead I braved the chair lift. I got on okay, but I was afraid to get off, so I decided to ride all the way around and get off and stay at the lodge. Instead, I tripped the rope and stopped the lift. I found out they don't let you ride all the way around.

"I was afraid to get off," I yelled to Richard, six feet below me. My feet were dangling, and 200 brightly colored ski parkas glared at me from the other side of the lift.

"Well, take your skis off and hop down," he said.

I hopped down and tried skiing down Fawn Trail. Halfway down, we took a wrong turn and ended up on North Face, the second hardest slope at the resort.

"I can't ski this. It's so steep that if I took a giant leap I'd fall straight down and land in front of the lodge without even touching the mountain."

"You can make it."

I did make it, after about two hundred falls. I spent the rest of the trip in our room.

Still, Richard had to have been a front-runner in the Trifecta during this time. We spent a lot of time together doing things *he* liked to do. When the weather was nice, I went golfing with him at the Country Club and accidentally whacked him in the shoulder when I was teeing off. He was telling me last minute instructions and inching forward to correct my stance; I decided to swing anyway. It was only a bruise.

I liked our "regular" dates—like basketball games. We saw the Pacers lose horrendously one night, but the evening was made enjoyable by the Elvis impersonator at half-time. I couldn't take my eyes off Elvis, mainly because I could have sworn he had on a hair T-shirt.

"Is that real hair or a hair T-shirt?" I said. "And where do they get those outfits? Think his mom is a seamstress?"

Richard ignored me. "Elvis" had on orange bell bottoms with white insert flares, an orange jacket with a gold-sequined trim, children's sunglasses, and a Roy Orbison wig. He had a white dish towel hung around his neck and sang "Love Me Tender." What price fame, I thought.

"What motivates him? Do you think he's humiliated? Do you think he feels like a star?" I said.

He shrugged.

Another night Richard and I went to see a modern dance troupe. When Richard would suggest dates like these, my first instinct was to cringe, but then they did seem different and inviting, so I went just to see.

"You never can tell," Tilly always said. "You might just like it."

Tilly made use accept every date that was offered. She once convinced me to go out with George Looper although he wore sandals, had a perm, worked as the Big Mac sauce-maker, didn't believe in God and wrote stories about lesbian vampires that lived in Washington, D.C. We had nothing in common, and he was an eyesore, but he sat next to me in Creative Writing and asked me out. "You never can tell," Tilly said. "While you're out with him, you might meet someone you like better," she said, as if at Jack Ensley's putt-putt I could tee off with another date and leave George at the 9th hole, as if at the movies I could sit next to and hold the hand of another, more attractive date. Just like that.

George showed up at the house in a T-shirt with his picture on the front, a new perm, and Jesus sandals. My mom had to run out of the room she was laughing so hard. I don't know what was more embarrassing, the T-shirt or the poncho he put on over it. We ate at McDonald's, and then went to a comic book convention where everyone looked and dressed like George. He never asked me out again.

Back to Richard. At the dance performance, men in tights pranced around the stage like drunken deer, while women in dresses made of rags looked haughty and tiptoed around the drunken deer. I was bored stiff.

Afterwards I convinced Richard to stop at the Bulldog. I needed to play some pool. I ran into Matt on my way to the bathroom, and he looked shocked.

"What?" I said.

"Nothing," he said. "I've just never seen you in the Bulldog with pantyhose on."

"I've been to see Dance Kaleidoscope."

"With Mr. Fortune Five Hundred?"

"Yes."

"Hmmm," he said.

"Hmmm what?"

"He just doesn't seem like your type."

"And who is my type?"

"Me," he said and laughed. "Just kidding."

"You're just a cultural clod while I," I said, "am refined."

And with that I caught my heel on a loose tile and stumbled to the bathroom. Matt had hit the nail on the head. He wasn't really my type. Richard wore tie clips and a London fog overcoat and pink cashmere sweaters. He carried a leather briefcase with his initials embossed in winking gold, and he wouldn't leave the house until Peter Jennings had given him the world picture. He didn't read the comics.

I read at least a book a week, didn't wear a lot of makeup, and wouldn't leave the house until Jeopardy was over, a game at which I beat Richard mercilessly. He was not impressed.

"Useless trivia," he said. "Nothing of importance."

My mind was a jukebox of useless trivia. I thrived on it.

"Fifty one percent of the women polled by Money magazine think about money more than sex," I told Richard during one particular lecture on economic implications of inflation. "One third actually prefer money over sex."

When he'd start with that small business venture, big capital investment malarkey, I'd search my jukebox for some pertinent fact.

"Did you read about that ex-con who made a fortune selling bait in a vending machine?"

More than anything, Sam hated what she called Richard's *alleged* intelligence. She claimed he sneered at her.

"My God," she said. "The man sells pantyhose for a living. Besides I can't imagine you married to someone named Dick."

Sam was disgusted with me during the time I dated Richard. She called me a "lapdog" and said I "kowtowed" to his every wish.

"Dance Kaleidoscope? Go on a real date," she said.

"Am I a lapdog?" I asked Trixie.

"Who cares?" Trixie said. "He's got money. He treats you good. You've got to kowtow to get what you want sometimes."

Tilly was the one to point out that although Richard had money, he was a spendthrift. Once when Richard was away on a pantyhose trip, I took Tilly by his townhouse to feed the cat. She took one look at his huge, hideous brown couch, and said she was beginning to have her doubts. The couch had big ruffled pillows with yellow and orange flowers stamped on them. It looked like a couch you'd have in a living room with a velveteen picture of those dogs playing poker, where the Bulldog is cheating.

"How come he dresses so nice and has a couch like this? It looks like it came from Sam Sablowsky's," she said.

"His mother buys all his clothes."

"Well, she better get her ass over here and decorate this house," she said. "I just can't picture you entertaining in a living room with that couch."

Richard's couch depressed Tilly for days. She just kept muttering and mulling over that couch. I was afraid she'd just come out and tell him.

When he came back, he brought me some daisies, and that pissed her off even more.

"Daisies," she said in the kitchen. "What are they? Three ninety-nine a bunch?"

But Richard was like my sister, and he could turn on the charm. Instead of going out that night, he suggested we stay home. We sat with Tilly on the porch drinking screwdrivers out of jars until three in the morning. Richard told Tilly how his Grandfather Folks had met his grandmother at a strawberry picking patch.

"She baked him a pie," he said. "Grandpa used to make moonshine."

"I always wanted to try some genuine moonshine," Tilly said. "You know your Paw Paw's cousin Billy went blind from moonshine. So they say."

Later I asked Tilly if she thought he was the one.

"I don't know," she said. "That couch.....But he does have nice dimples, and you'd probably have beautiful children," she added trying to figure if beautiful children balanced out the ugly couch. She definitely had not made up her mind.

"Frank's coming back in town," she added nonchalantly. "And I saw Matt at the Bingo parlor."

"Frank?" I said. It figured Tilly knew before I did that Frank was coming home. "How do you know?"

"I just got a feeling. And I think something important will

happen at Emma's wedding. You really should make up your mind by then."

Tilly said make up my mind as if I were shopping for a new dress—instead of a husband. Was getting married that easy? Richard said he liked me a lot and wanted me to meet his family. That seemed like a good sign. Frank was coming home, or so Tilly said. That seemed like a good sign. And then there was Matt. I pictured him playing darts, his tan, muscular legs and his perfectly filled out Bermudas. "Bullseye," I said.

I had known Matt all my life. Or so it seemed. At 8, he advised me on Christmas shopping. "If you want to get a lot of presents for Christmas, leave celery for the reindeers," he confided. "Reindeers like celery."

I remembered accompanying Matt on his yearly shopping sprees to Haag's drugs. Although my mom wouldn't let me cross the street by myself until I was thirteen, she did let me walk with Matt to Haag's. I guess he was a dependable enough guardian. Matt did all his Christmas shopping there, and one year he bought his dad a bottle of Aqua Velva in the shape of a construction worker that he was especially proud of.

"Look," he showed me, "the hat screws off."

"Neat," I said.

"I do all my shopping here. You can too. You can get all your presents for five, maybe ten bucks."

Once or twice, if he couldn't find anyone else, he even let me go fishing with him. We'd walk over to the swamp, and I would proudly put my worm on myself. I grew up fishing with my dad. If he was impressed he never said. To him, fishing was a serious business. Afterwards, we'd walk by Dairy Queen and get a dipped cone, Dutch treat.

On family vacations, Matt toured all of the historical sites in the area. Matt knew where the first Coke bottle was made in Indiana. He had seen the Liberty Bell, visited a museum dedicated to General Custer, peered off Pike's Peak, and sat on Plymouth Rock. I remember him coming home from vacation every year, from Niagara Falls, from the caves of Kentucky, from witch-ridden homes in New England with the same disgusted look on his face. "I'd rather have just gone fishing," he said.

We stayed friends all through high school and during college. At college, Matt wrote me of nurses that wanted to give him backrubs, of rugby parties where they allegedly had nude human bowling and of plans he had. "I want to have my own fishing show. Like Babe Winkleman," he wrote.

I outlined my college beaux, parties and plans in equal detail. "I met the Carolina baseball team," I wrote. "I want to work for a magazine in New York City," I said. "And I want to be tan all year around." From these college castles in the sky, we'd both returned home.

It was hard to believe that someone who used his beach towel to capture birds in the trash cans at the swim pool and then tied strings around the birds' legs (or at least claimed to) and flew them like kites (or at least claimed to) was now a college graduate and working man. Matt was an engineer and was dating a girl he'd met at the dentist's office. She was pale and petite, a regular china doll. The first time I met her, I wanted to squash her like a bug.

I don't know why I had Matt on my mind when it was Richard who appeared to be on the hook. Richard asked me to Chicago to meet his family, and I accepted.

Richard's mother was one of those perfect 50's Moms. She used to bake gingerbread men for Christmas class parties and cupcakes in the shape of hearts for Valentine's Day. Her famous Halloween cake was shaped like a ghost and had Peppermint Patties for eyes. When all her kids went off to school, a high school friend and she opened a yarn shop that was successful.

As a thank-you-for-the-visit gift, I had attempted to cross-stitch a kitchen sampler that hung in a plastic frame. I ended up super gluing the felt for the back of the frame to my finger. I sat picking the dried felt off my finger, while he was doing the French knots for the baby blanket I was making for my sister.

"So you and Rich spend quite a lot of time together," she

said.

I shrugged, embarrassed.

"I feel for you," she said. "He's just like his father. So domineering. So particular. As a kid, Richard wouldn't eat his peanut butter and jelly sandwiches unless they were cut a certain way. They had to be cut with a sharp knife so that there were no jagged edges. Each half pinched together.

"He used to rate my lunches on to four. A four used to be Campbell's tomato soup, a bologna sandwich cut in fours, and milk. Then he decided this lacked originality, so one day he came home and announced he wanted liverwurst. I don't know where he picked that up at, but I bought him liverwurst, and he ate it. Poor thing. He would have given his right arm for plain old bologna."

"I'm a pretty picky eater," I said.

"Does he make you eat new foods?"

I nodded. The night before he said, "She will have crabs." I hated when he ordered for me. Plus when I cracked a crab open and something green slid out. I said I wasn't hungry and ate oyster crackers.

"Well don't kowtow to him," she said. "Once you start kowtowing, you'll be doing it for the rest of your life. Unless you wait to rebel when they're too old to care. Like me."

Richard had two brothers—one worked as a mechanic in a motorcycle shop in Wyoming. I saw a picture of him on the mantle—he had a pony tail, wore a Corona T-shirt, and was missing part of his front tooth. I couldn't picture him standing next to Richard in his pink cashmere sweater, I couldn't imagine them in the same family. Richard hadn't spoken with his brother since Christmas.

"You don't talk to him on a regular basis?" I said.

"No, we have nothing in common," he said.

"But he's your brother."

The other brother was an insurance salesman, married to an ex-cheerleader, Sally, who looked ill at ease without her pompoms. They had two boys. I hated Sally on sight. She was the type that said things like, "Nice dress. Did you make it?" She said something to me, along the lines of, "I love the natural look—no set hairstyle or makeup—no boring color scheme to stick to in your wardrobe." I wished Sam was with me to think of something catty to say back. Instead, I smiled and acted and felt like a hillbilly.

That night Richard had tickets to see the symphony. I said I didn't want to go. In fact, I wanted to go home. I said I'd rather go to a jazz club and have a few beers.

"You drink too much," he said.

I stuck my tongue out, chugged a big sip, and burped. He looked disgusted.

"Get dressed," he said, handing me a new pair of pantyhose.

I threw them back at him. I realized that didn't want to put on the pantyhose. I felt like I was rehearsing for a part I wasn't sure I wanted to play. Richard had all the qualities of a good husband—I'd be a fool to pass him up. He was hardworking and would be a good provider, handy around the house even. He changed the oil in my car, helped me work out a budget, and advised me on what brand stereo to buy. He wanted children, and he seemed like he would be a good father, at least he was great with his nephews. He was nice looking; heads turned when he entered the room. He was Catholic, and he even went to Mass. I couldn't figure out what was missing.

Chapter 8

But For the Grace of God

Usually summer was Tilly's favorite part of the year, mainly because I was either home from school, when I was younger, or off from school, when I started teaching. She and I would spend the entire summer together going to the pool, getting our hair done, trying out different happy hours, just enjoying being together. Paw Paw died when I was 16 and Tilly moved in with us then, although she kept her house in Oldenburg. Her room and my room were right next to each other. Since Jess's funeral and Tilly's bout in the hospital, I made it a habit to listen at her door for her breathing or her snoring and to check on her to make sure she hadn't fallen out of bed. Tilly was always wrestling with someone in her dreams, the person she described as the "Man with the Umbrella" that she said was coming to get her.

Usually she was awake, scouting around for some chocolate or listening for mice. Tilly was terrified of mice, and I hated birds. We had a sort of running war. As a joke, I'd hide little furry things in her Kleenex box or in the pocket of her robe so that when she put her hand in, she'd feel my furry surprise.

At the pool, she'd get me back by lining the crust of her grilled cheese in a path to my feet. The bold birds would nibble closer and closer, and I'd scream, grab my hair, and run, flapping my arms as if I were the one that could fly away.

This time instead of filling her in on my latest date, I got to hear about *her* hot date. Tilly always complained about having only one man all her life. She said she wanted a new husband—one with a yacht. "If I'd of known your Paw Paw was going to die and leave me, I would have set something up earlier," she said. It was all hogwash. Tilly had plenty of opportunities, and she skittered away like a scared colt.

She had two suitors that called her all the time. One was bald, had a naked woman tattooed on his leg, and kept his teeth in a jar under the car seat of his custom made Cadillac. His name was Joey. The other one had known my grandmother in high school and claimed my grandfather stole her away from him. His name was Duke, and he had his first wife's name, Florence, tattooed on his hands. A letter on each knuckle. Duke was never even a contender, especially after I listened in on the last phone call from him. But Joey was kind of fun.

He was a great card player, and he had a condominium in Florida. He called on a Thursday and took Til to the Slippery Noodle for beers. When I came in that night, I listened at her door for her snoring. Just as I leaned into the door, she snatched it open.

"Gotcha."

I hopped in the air and grabbed my heart, much to her delight, genuinely gotten.

"Okay, you got me. What are you doing up?"

She was standing in her lampshade cap holding a curtain rod like a cane.

"I'm the Pied Piper," she told me. "I'm leading the mice to your room. Go to RaeAnn's room."

"What?"

"Seriously," she said, "there's something in my closet."

"I know. It's the mice."

"All the food lying around here, it's no wonder we have mice," she said. "Our mice went down to the canal and got all their relations. Told them all the delicious food we have here. And they all moved in."

"Well, whose plate with left over pie crumbs is that?" I said.

"Mine."

"And whose baggie with half a pastrami sandwich?"

"Mine."

"And whose bowl of ice cream is the hallway?"

"Oh, that's your father's. Speaking of your father," she said, "go see if he has that bag of Snickers by his bed. I'm hungry."

I snuck into my parents room and spotted a bag of M&M's next to my dad's head. He was snoring away. Just as I touched the bag of candy, his internal alarm went off.

"Don't touch those," he said without opening his eyes.

I jumped for the second time that night. "They're for Tilly," I said.

"Okay, then."

I crept back into Tilly's room, pulled back her curtains, took two beers from the six-pack lined on the window sill, and opened them. We drank beer and ate M&M's.

"How was your hot date?" I said.

"Don't even think about it. He doesn't even have any teeth."

"Yes, he does. He just doesn't wear them."

"He sure looked old. It was obvious I had held up better than him, and he was proud of me. You should have seen him in the Slippery Noodle showing me off. It was embarrassing."

"Did he tell you that you still look like Alice Faye?" I said. Tilly said everyone used to think she looked like Alice Faye, the movie star. I have a picture of her propped up against the sideboard of a car, showing a little leg. That's how I picture Alice Faye to look.

She smiled. "No."

"He seems like a nice guy. What's the matter with him?"

"He doesn't have a yacht. I always said my next one would have a yacht."

"Well, if you played your cards right, I'm sure he'd get you one."

"That old fart? The total cost of every piece of furniture in his living room was about three hundred dollars. He couldn't afford a yacht."

"He afforded that car. Hey, wait a minute. You went to his house? You didn't tell me you went to his house."

"Shithead. You sound like a shithead as usual."

"Besides, he's got a condo."

"Hell, it's not *on the beach*. It's in town," she said. "Piss on it if it's not on the beach. Besides, why do you want to pawn me off on some old fart with no teeth. I hope your Paw Paw is watching all of this."

"Well, what are you dinging about getting a man for then? What are you looking for?"

"Someone like Paw Paw."

"Paw Paw didn't have a yacht or any teeth."

"Someone like Paw Paw with a yacht and teeth. Besides, we can't be worrying about me. We've got to get someone to take you first," she said. "Just exactly what are you looking for?"

"Someone like Paw Paw."

Tilly accepted that answer. "Great minds run in the same channel."

Then she got serious. "I'm worried about you. As a matter of fact, I'm worried about both of us. At the rate we're going there won't be anyone at your wedding or my funeral. We'll have to *hire* people to fill the church. For Christmas next year, I'd like to see you with a fiancé."

"What brought that on?" I said. "Your date?"

Tilly paused and looked out the window. "When we were out, we ran into some old friends that knew your Paw Paw from his filling station. They told me Lefty Williams died the other day. And Eloise's daughters finally put her in the nursing home. And Duke is getting married."

"Lefty Williams? Your first love? The one Dottie Michaels stole from you?"

"Yep," she said. "He always did have a thing for me. Why, he could have been your grandfather. Lucky for you I picked Paw Paw."

Lefty was one of Tilly's first suitors, and the first, and probably only man, to break her heart. I guess he invited Tilly on a hayride, but her father wouldn't let her go. Her best friend, Dottie, went though, and on the fated hayride, Dottie stole Lefty from Tilly.

I could just picture Tilly with her bloomers on. "We wore bloomers back then," she told me. "Blue during the week and white on Sundays." I could picture her sitting on her front porch wishing she was on the hayride. Her sister Katie would probably be sneaking out a window to go anyway, but Tilly would listen to her dad. Since her mother died just after Tilly's youngest brother was born, her dad raised Tilly and her sister and three brothers alone during the Depression.

"Not only did Dottie steal Lefty, but she ruined my feet, too," Tilly said. Then she explained, "I wasn't allowed to have high heels," she said. "But I wanted some really bad, so Dottie and I walked to the store and bought five cents worth of sugar. We went to her house, baked some cookies, and sold them out front. With the money we made, we went to a second-hand store and bought some high heels. Mine were a size too small. No wonder my feet are in this condition," she said.

"Enough about me. I've had my man. What about you? Did you meet anyone interesting? Any husband material?" she asked.

"No. "

"Well, who did you see?"

"I saw Matt. He was with some wench. A tiny little thing."

"That five-foot-two, eyes-of-blue one?"

"Yeah."

"You could knock her silly."

"I know," I said. "Anyway, he said we shouldn't use cheese in the mousetraps because that's a fallacy that mice like cheese. He said to use caramel because the mice like it, and when they eat it, it gets stuck in their teeth. They can't breath, so they die."

"You told him we had mice?" she said. Then as an afterthought she added, "I wish I had some caramel."

She contemplated either caramel or some other idea for a few seconds.

"What about this Matt? I've always liked him."

"We're just friends."

"Love is friendship caught fire," she said.

"Besides he's already got a woman."

Tilly raised her eyebrows and sipped her beer.

The next day I took her to the nursing home to visit her friend Eloise. I hated the nursing home. It smelled like urine and rotting teeth. At the entrance, some man begged us to take him to the Watch Repair Shop in Mishawaka.

"It's my heart," he explained. "It's stopped, but they'll fix it there. I'll give you a buck."

When we got to the nursing home, it was lunchtime, so we rolled Eloise into the cafeteria to her exact spot, at Table 1. Seats in nursing homes are the power brokers. Only important people sat at the first tables to be served, and everyone sat in their exact spot, Eloise explained to us. You could get pronged with a fork or batted with a cane if you took someone else's place, for everyone knew if your seat in the cafeteria was gone, you'd soon follow.

For one week Eloise lived with the oldest person in the United States. It seemed Clarence Pfeiffer from Scranton, Pennsylvania, formerly the oldest, died, passing his crown on to Esther Matheny, Eloise's roommate. Esther was 112 years five months old.

The mayor proclaimed Esther Matheny Day, and Esther got a new shawl and corsage. The news crew came to interview her, but she wouldn't say a thing. She just sat there chewing her gums and blinking her eyes. Our neighbor did, though. She smiled at the camera and said, "I don't want any more of that goddamn corn pudding."

Esther reigned for three and a half weeks before she died passing the world's oldest crown onto a man in St. Paul, Minnesota.

After we got Eloise situated at her lunch table, a lady started pounding on the table.

"Move me to my seat. This isn't my seat. I've been here twelve years, and I've always sat at Table Four." She pointed to a woman with a purple crocheted shawl on her shoulders. "That bitch is in my seat," she screamed. "Move her."

The attendant calmly explained and pointed to the big red sign on the table that said Table 4. The woman insisted she was at the wrong table. Finally, she broke down sobbing—the attendant—not the woman. Another attendant came in, wheeled the woman around the room, brought her back to the same table, and said, "See, Table Four." The woman smiled.

Next they wheeled in a man with a tweed cap, and Eloise waved to him.

"There's one of my boyfriends," she told Tilly and waved eagerly at him.

Tilly and I exchanged looks. When my grandma Jess was in the nursing home, she claimed to have four boyfriends. Then it was down to three. She told us that one died and wanted to be buried on top of Louie, her one and only husband. Another time she said she had triplets. "What did you do with them?" my dad asked. "I gave them away," Grandma said. "I was ashamed of them."

In the cafeteria, Eloise's boyfriend started pointing at his penis and singing "Roll out the barrel, we'll have a barrel of fun. Roll out the barrel, we'll have a barrel of fun. Roll out the barrel, we'll have a barrel of fun" until one of the other patients beaned him in the head with a roll.

"He's awful young, isn't he?" Tilly said.

"Not for me, he isn't."

"Why, Eloise. What do you do with all those boyfriends?"

"Why, Tilly," Eloise replied, exasperated. "you screw 'em!" She looked to her lunch companion for confirmation. "Isn't that right. You screw 'em."

Her companion smiled, burbled a reply, and spit something orange across the table.

Tilly shrugged. "Sally Crossey's mother kept telling her she had a burning 'down there.' They found out she had stuck a tube of Ben Gay up herself."

"Sheesh," Eloise said. "I'm kidding. I'd go insane in here if it wasn't for my sense of humor. Only thing is no one gets my jokes."

She smiled weakly and then turned her head and looked out the window. I saw Tilly roll up and stick out her tongue, which she always does when she's about ready to cry.

The man at the next table was pointing at a pregnant girl standing with him and yelling, "Who's the fat girl? Who's the fat girl? "

"That's your granddaughter dear," his wife replied. "She's pregnant."

"Well, what's she going," he said, "an elephant?"

The wife smiled. "We're going to be going now, dear. I'll be back later."

"Well, leave me a couple of bucks for a beer," he grumbled.

"He thinks he's at a hotel," his wife said to us.

We said good-bye to Eloise and walked to our car.

"But for the grace of God," Tilly said and crossed herself.

Tilly had played such a big part in my life. As she watched all of her friends get old and sick and crazy, I noticed how she fretted over what lay ahead for her. I worried about her a lot and watched her closely. I didn't realize at the time that she was worrying about me and watching me.

She got a phone call from Duke one afternoon, and he invited her to his wedding. She didn't want him imagining that she was upset, which she was indeed not, so she made me go with her. The wedding was held in the basement of Margie's sisters church on the Southside. The floor was covered with black and white tile. The wall was made of cinder blocks. I couldn't think of a more depressing place to get married. Banners made of felt hung around the rim of the ceiling. One said, "Thou art dust and to dust you shall return."

Tilly and I made our way through the steel folding chairs and found a seat. There were lots of old women with hankies there.

"Duke must have made the rounds," I said.

Tilly rolled her eyes. She looked like a beauty queen compared to the other old women there. She had just had her hair frosted a golden silver and wore a new pink suit. Her skin was smooth and wrinkle-free. Her blue eyes were sharp and told me a hundred things with one look.

"You look nice," I said.

Duke was grinning up in front in a white polyester suit, a big polka dotted bow tie, and white shoes. Tilly started laughing when she saw him.

"See," she said. "I told you he looks like an embalmed Porky Pig. He's even got on Porky Pig's bow tie."

Margie entered from what looked like a storage closet. She wore a big floppy hat, a blue polyester dress with what looked like Easter lilies swirling along in the fabric, and knee-hi support hose. Tilly leaned up in her seat and stared long and hard at Margie. I figured she was imagining what it'd be like if she were wearing the big floppy wedding hat.

She sat back. "That's not Margie," she whispered.

"What do you mean? Maybe she looks different in a hat?"

"That's not Margie," she said loudly.

The ceremony was short. The minister must have figured

they didn't have much time for pomp and circumstance, so he just joined their hands and declared them married. Then there was a toast with sparkling apple juice, and everyone was invited to partake in cookies and a congratulatory embrace from the newlyweds. Tilly and I took our place in line.

"This is my wife Cecile," Duke said proudly.

"What happened to Margie?" Tilly said.

"She died," Duke said and took the hand of the next person in line, his smile never faltering.

I looked at Tilly. Her eyebrows were knitted together, and her tongue was rolled up and stuck out. She was definitely thinking hard about something.

"But for the grace of God," I said to no one in particular.

Early the next morning I heard Tilly screaming and thought that she was asleep and dreaming about the man with the umbrella coming to get her. She always had the same nightmare about a man with an umbrella, standing outside the window. "He's here to get me," she'd cry. "It's the man with the umbrella."

When I went into the hallway, a bird shot past me and touched my hair. I screamed and crawled on my hands and knees into Tilly's room. I stood up and slammed the door.

"It's a bird," Tilly said and kind of laughed. "What should we do?"

"We have to get him out of the house?" I screamed.

"But how? "

"I'm certainly not," I said. "You know me and birds."

"Well, we can't stay in this room all day," Tilly said. "I've got a doctor's appointment."

"Let's call Mom."

What my mother, who was at work, could do for a bird in our house, I didn't know. But we called her, and she had the nerve to laugh. Then she called our 92-year old neighbor, who came over with a fly swatter, hit the bird dead, carried him out by one wing, and dumped him in the trash. I was in awe.

"A bird in the house," Tilly said.

I finished the sentence in my head—a bird in the house means a death in the family.

Chapter 9

The Professor

At Tilly's advice, I went to see a fortuneteller to see what prospects she could foresee. Richard had sent me flowers after our tiff in Chicago, but I was putting him off, mainly because Tilly said Frank would be home. I was anxious to see whether he was really coming home. I was both excited and scared to see him.

The fortuneteller, Mississippi, had her office in half a beauty shop. The place smelled like cats and perm fluid and made me nervous. I had never met this woman, so when she greeted me at the door with a Woody Woodpecker hair-do—same style and color—I was not only nervous. I was scared.

Mississippi escorted me into a separate section of the house. She took my money and placed it in a drawer full of ten-dollar bills. She sat in a rocking chair, ran her fingers through her flaming red hair, and rolled her eyes back in her head.

"I see on the light side of heaven," she said. "It's like watching TV."

The first thing she told me was that I was waiting for a phone call from the West. California she thought. She said he would call tomorrow. She was right. Tilly had said that Frank was coming home. I was hoping he'd come in town in time to escort me to Emma and Eric's wedding.

"What will the caller tell me?" I said.

"He's coming home."

What a relief, I thought to myself. Then I asked Mississippi, "What kind of future do I have with this caller?"

"I see you walking down an aisle. There are three men at the altar, and he's one of them. You will marry one of them."

"Which one? Who are the others?"

"One has on a pink cummerbund."

That must be Richard I thought to myself.

"And one is wearing Red Chuck Taylor's."

I was amazed that her TV reception was good enough to see the brand of tennis shoes.

"And one is stepping forward."

Just as one stepped forward I guess she had technical difficulties or something because she couldn't tell me which one I was going to marry.

Just as Tilly predicted, Frank did come in town. Sam called to tell me the news.

"Shreve saw Frank at the Alley Cat on Tuesday night," she said.

"And it's Friday, and he hasn't even called me," I said. "I give up on him."

The wedding to rival weddings, Enema's and Earache's, was only weeks away, and I didn't have much time to make Frank take me. I decided to sweat it out and let him call me first.

"There's always Richard," I said.

"How about Matt?" Tilly said.

"He's got a girlfriend."

I slunk around the house praying for a miracle. Frank came over the next day. Just like usual, he came in, opened the refrigerator, and popped a beer. My mom hustled downstairs as if he were there to see her.

"Don't start, Darla. Just don't start," he said. "I have one word to say to you—Bullshit."

My mom giggled and called him Frances.

After Darla, Frank went in to say hello to Ray, and they immediately started planning their next fishing trip.

"Hell," Frank said. "Let's go today." His first visit, and he made a date with my dad. I knew I would be ignored when they started discussing bait.

"Crickets," Frank said. "I tell you, Ray, that's why we never caught any. We need some crickets."

My dad called Frank "Professor." Of all the times they went fishing, they never caught a thing—at least not any keepers.

"They're out of season," Daddy said.

"I bet we could find someone around here who still has

some. Hey, RaeAnn, can you do your dad a favor? Call up that bait and tackle shop on Fall Creek and tell them we need some crickets."

I called the bait shop for them, got them some crickets, and off they went. When they got home, Daddy said, "The Professor took me to a *good* fishing hole today."

"How many did you catch?"

Frank interrupted. "Oh, they were biting okay."

"Where are they?"

"Well," he said. "We threw them back. You know the theory of catch and release. Why, if Ray and I kept all the fish we caught, there wouldn't be a fish left in Indiana for anyone else. Isn't that right?"

"You're the Professor."

"Bullshit, Frank," Mom said.

I waited for him to pull out his newspaper clipping. When challenged, Frank proved his fishing ability with a newspaper clipping.

"Look at this, Darla. It's printed right here in the *Indianapolis Star* with my very own face and the fish I caught— a record! And he wasn't even the biggest one I caught that day. I caught his big brother, but I had to throw him back."

He waited for us to ask why. We'd heard it before.

"See, I had to throw it back because there wasn't room in the boat for both me and him."

"Bullshit, Frank."

I smirked because I knew the true story of that fish clipping. Frank was infatuated with Lynne and got drunk enough one night to tell her that he bought the state-record fish at Florida's Fish Market. Loose lips, sink ships, and Lynne got drunk and told me. I didn't have the heart to tell him I knew, but I laughed even harder every time he pulled it out.

Frank and I had had some fun times, mostly in his big blue van with the trout painted on the side of it. It had one seat—the driver's seat. Everyone else who went out in the van had to bring his own chair. We'd go by and pick up all his friends and their lawn chairs and go play darts. We never went out alone. I did get the prime seat of co-pilot in the van, but only because I had a heavy rod iron lawn chair that wouldn't slide when we turned a corner. One night, Tom Reilly passed out got so tangled up in his fold-out chair from sliding around that we had to leave him in the van overnight.

In Indianapolis, you hung out at one of three bars: The Dog, the Cat, or the Mouse. Our group favored the Bulldog. But Frank's friends went to the Alley Cat. They had real darts at the Alley Cat, an owner who looked like Al Capone and who often forgot it was closing time, and an old lady that played the piano and sang tunes. Tilly, Mom and Aunt Kay, all hung out at the Alley Cat during their heyday.

I was a pretty good dart player, and Frank and I usually won, despite his nagging. We only won because, although I wasn't aiming at them, I'd hit some pretty high scores, and then he'd take care of the precision work to get us out. He also coached me at euchre, talking the entire game.

"It's going to be a loner. I feel it coming. This is it RaeAnn. A loner. I'm dealing myself a loner. Four points and we're out of the game." If I played against him, I heard, "You're going to eat that one. Did I hear you call hearts?." He'd sniff the air. "Do I smell a euchre?"

He took me fishing, when my dad wasn't available.

"Cast over here," he coached. "You'll have better luck."

" I don't exactly see you reeling them in," I said.

"Do I have to get the clipping out to prove I know what I'm talking about. Cast over here."

I cast the other way, and I caught a 5 1/2-pound bass.

"Look at this," I said. "I've never caught a fish this big. It's a good one, isn't it?"

"It's not so bad," he said inspecting it. "I've seen better. I told you you'd catch a good one if you cast by that tree. Why, I think I taught you everything you know about fishing."

"For your information," I said, "I've been fishing with my dad since I was six." I took the fish off the hook by myself and threw it back. I thought he was going to dive in after it.

"Daddy taught me everything," I said.

"Oh yeah, who taught you to bait a hook?"
"My dad."
"To take a fish off the hook?"
"Daddy."
"Well, I taught you to tie a hook on."
"Matt Tyler did, in third grade."

He also took me squirrel hunting, although I didn't see a squirrel all day. I did hit the Pepsi can we used for target practice. The second time we went dove hunting, and I shot a black bird. The third time, he left me home. He had a very tight agenda and a million friends, and I was left home more than I liked.

"The boys are going. You can come later to the cook out. We'll make bunny stew."

We did make bunny stew. Frank made a spit with two Y-shaped sticks and a straight one and cooked the rabbit over a little fire. He brought along a pot, some water, a potato and a carrot. I brought two beef bullion cubes and some whiskey.

"What are you going to do this summer and next fall?" I said when I was going away to college.

"I'm going where the wind takes me."

"Really, have you applied to any colleges?"

"Harvard, Yale, Notre Dame," he said. "I just can't decide."

"How about a football scholarship?"

"Did I tell you I can play Tripe Face Boogie on the guitar? Listen."

"What about me?" I said.

He strummed his guitar. "Stick with me, baby, and you'll be wearing diamonds."

I packed up for college. And the one unforgivable thing that Frank did—besides not saying good-bye—was make arrangements for the trailer my dad used to take me to college.

"Don't waste your money renting a U-Haul," Frank said. "I can set you up with a real fine trailer of a friend of mine."

So instead of renting a U-Haul like I begged, my dad borrowed a trailer Frank's friend had made. I'll never forget it—it looked like an outhouse. And if that wasn't bad enough, the muffler came off the Grand Am on our way through the mountains. Frank had tuned up the car. Here I was a freshman in college, trying to move into my dorm with some dignity, feeling like the Beverly Hillbillies, hearing that car coming for miles, and then seeing it pull into the dorm's circled drive with that outhouse strapped on the back.

The Motor Club had booked us at the Downtowner, a supposedly AAA rated hotel. Old veterans lurked around the coffee shop. Young veterans hung out in the bar. My dad asked the bartender where the bathroom was, and he pointed to a door. My dad opened it, fell down a flight of stairs, and broke three ribs. We had to drive him through downtown on a Saturday night with that outhouse dragging behind us and him moaning.

I cried like crazy when they started to leave me, and my mom said, "That's it Ray. Pack her stuff back up. We're taking her home." But I stayed.

Frank moved to California right after everyone left for college. I didn't hear from him until a week before his birthday in October. He called me collect at school and told me that if I were planning on sending him a birthday present, he sure would appreciate some socks.

"What are you doing out there?" I said.

"Making my millions."

"He's selling children's encyclopedia's door-to-door," his sister told me. "He's making a fortune. Really. He sent my mom his first check."

"He's delivering sheets to cabins in Yosemite Park," Sam told me. He called Shreve and invited him out. "Said the fishing was incredible."

"He's putting ceilings into shopping malls," Matt told me. "He's making good money, though. And he lives with some forty-year old with a swimming pool. She just bought him a new motorcycle."

While he was away, I wrote him long letters, and occasionally I'd be surprised with a letter back. He'd always include a little goodie: a Batman Pez candy dispenser, a 5-by-7-inch glossy picture of himself, a packet of root beer bubble bath, and a charm in the shape of a bottle opener.

The only time I ever saw him was at Christmas. He came in

town every Christmas, and we went to midnight mass. "I'm home for good this time," he told me every year. Then a couple weeks later, I'd call his house, and his mom would say he'd left last night. "Can't let any grass grow under his feet," she said.

I wouldn't hear from him until he ran out of socks.

Chapter 10

Mining for Gold

I was glad Frank was in town, and we quickly got into our usual routine. We'd make plans, and he'd show up 50% of the time. My mom reminded me of all of his no-shows.

"Remember when he was going to take you to the Indy 500. He called you and gave you a list of what to bring."

"Ten submarine sandwiches and a batch of brownies," I said and rolled my eyes.

"You packed up that cooler with everything you needed. And sat on the front porch and waited. And waited."

"Yes, I remember," I said. "I finally gave up around ten and ate two subs and the entire batch of brownies."

"That was a good one," mom said.

I gave her a dirty look. I didn't know why she liked that story so much.

"Remember when he was supposed to help clean out the farm?" Tilly said.

"Yes," I said.

"Who did end up helping your dad with that?" mom said.

"Matt."

When my grandfather died, my dad had to put Jess in a nursing home because she required constant medical care. When their money started running out, he had to sell the farm to keep her in the nursing home. They leveled the house and put up cheap apartments. My dad salvaged everything he could.

Matt and I helped him bring home all the doors from the house, signs that said "Fresh Eggs" from the barn, all of my grandfather's gadgets, the riding lawn mower, mattresses, old pillows, scrapbooks, silverware, and a house full of furniture. He even had an old cabinet from the kitchen removed and brought it home. He couldn't bear to part with anything, so be brought it all home and stored it at our house. At one time, we had 13 dressers. Cabinets lined the rooms. Mattresses sat stacked across the back porch. Boxes of broken kitchen appliances, sterling silver, and chipped dishes were piled in a kitchen corner.

"Don't throw that away," Daddy would yell if you touched anything. "Ma used to make strawberry pie in that pan." Or he'd say "That's a perfectly good blender. It's just broken, but I'm going to fix it" "Leave that sign alone. I used to hang that sign out to sell corn."

Probably his favorite acquisition was his dad's riding lawn mower. On the wide expanse of the farm, Daddy loved to mow the lawn. Although our yard far from required a riding lawn mower, he insisted on perching on the mower and using it to cut our relatively small lawn. I could picture him trying to maneuver around the yard, forwarding and reversing around the strawberry barrel and tulip trees. Exhausted from steering, my dad would come inside, leaving the yard looking like a cheap haircut, cowlicks of grass erratically jumping up all over.

The back yard was especially hard to mow because of my dad's, probably inherited, inclination towards gadgets. He had his boat collection: a Sears fishing boat filled with every known fishing and boating apparatus that would fit, a depth finder, captain seat, trolling motor, regular motor, deluxe model tackle box, depth finder, running lights; a ski boat that didn't work, and a motor attached to a barrel of water that my dad periodically started up and watched whirling water around the backyard.

He also had his garden collection, a green thumb apparently not being one of the things he inherited from his parents. He had a barren strawberry barrel, a vegetable patch choked with weeds, and a rocked off section housing his flowers, none bloomed. His cooking collection dotted the backyard: a grill he built of stone and abandoned for a charcoal grill, a charcoal grill he abandoned for a gas grill, and a gas grill. Various spatulas, meat forks, plates were sprinkled between the grills. Add to this lawn chairs, a picnic table, a plastic pool filled with green water and a plastic turtle filled with sand. My dad finally gave up mowing the grass. Most of it was covered by some gadget anyway.

Not only was the backyard filled with gadgets, my dad also had other collections stored in the basement, including his frame-making, dollhouse-making equipment, his old train set, and boxes full of costumes, practical joke props, and items he'd purchased from late night TV ads and mail order catalogues.

He just could not resist those TV ads. In his sleep, he would hear an ad on late night TV for the complete record set of Patsy Cline, and he'd wake up and call. Every week or so a mysterious package would appear in the mail.

"What's that?" I'd ask.

"That's mine," Daddy would say and then he'd sneak upstairs to open his latest treasure in secret.

The basement was a treasure trove of things. He had a plastic ass with lip marks you could strap on; he had a Dracula costume he wore to school during Halloween to delight the first graders. He had a naked boy liquor dispenser, a statue of St. Peter in the shape of a penis, a bullhorn, and a talking toilet seat that caused my Aunt Kay to knock her front tooth out. When she sat down and heard someone say, "I'm working down here," she jumped up, fell forward in her tangle of pants, and knocked her tooth out. My dad felt terrible.

Frank's latest no-show was reminiscent of the farm outing because he promised he'd help clean out our basement, which now stored all the farm stuff, plus all our junk from years gone by.

"I've got just the truck for it, Ray," he told my dad. "Don't hire someone to haul that stuff away. You'd be throwing money away. I can help you get it all cleaned out, and plus, I know that basement is a gold mine. A gold mine," he stressed. "I wouldn't miss it for the world."

Of course, he didn't show up. It was Lynne's idea to clean out the basement. She insisted it be done immediately, and because she was due in the next month or so, we humored her. She came over and directed the operation.

"What made you come up with this brilliant idea?" I said in a whiny voice.

"We'll have to do it sometime," she said. "Just think how sad we'd be if we waited until they died."

I guess she'd been thinking about someone dying, too. We thought there was no way to ward off this unlucky cycle, so we bided our time and worried about everyone, Tilly especially.

"I don't think I'd be sad," I said looking around at the thirty some odd years of junk piled in the basement. "I think I'd be pissed. Plus, I still like my idea better. If and when we have to sell the house, we can just board up the basement and act like the house doesn't even have one. No one would ever have to know."

"This will be fun, girls," mom said. "Think of all the memories."

Mom sat on a box and went through things—deciding what could be thrown away, trying to pawn off items on Lynne and I, and reminiscing. I hauled boxes upstairs and out to the front yard, making a pile out front.

Among the items we found in the basement were green beans canned by Grandma Jess who'd been dead for almost a year and in the nursing home for at least 10 years before that and probably hadn't canned in 20 years before that. The jars reminded me of a jar from biology class—an aborted puppy swimming in formaldehyde, its pink eyes scrunched closed. I picked up a spinach can and swore it moved.

"Remember that grub worm Tilly ate," I said.

We once almost owned the Lite beer company. Before Miller made Lite, another company made a Lite beer, and mom and Tilly claimed they were going to shrink away to nothing drinking this low-calorie beer. But then Tilly swallowed a grub worm from one of the bottles. Then we were going to have millions when we sued the company.

We hired a lawyer. I couldn't remember if Tilly spit up the grub worm, and they used that for evidence. Or maybe she just described the feeling of swallowing it. "I knew it was a grub worm. I can tell by the way it felt sliding down my throat." She must have not been very convincing because we never did get any money out of it.

Half the stuff in the basement was rotten. We had to use a shovel to remove Lynne's knitting machine—it had rotted to the shelf. We found my rock polishing kit, my creepy crawler kit, my fuzzy pumper hairstyling set, Lynne's cartoon drawing kit, board games, old art projects, and moldy baby dolls.

"This was your favorite doll," Mom said. "Remember Poor Pitiful Pearl."

I remembered when I'd cry mom would call me Poor Pitiful Pearl, but I didn't remember any doll.

"Pitch it," I said.

"We're not pitching Poor Pitiful Pearl. It's probably a collector's item," she said.

"Her eyes are moldy," Lynne said.

"I'll clean it," Mom said and set it back on the shelf.

"Here's our Barbie clothes," Lynne said, opening a suitcase of Barbie clothes my mom had sewn for us. When we were growing up, we had the coolest Barbie clothes. Mom sewed fur-trimmed jackets and sequin evening gowns and business suits and full-skirted party dresses.

"Mom, you made the best stuff," I said. "The girls will go wild when they see this stuff."

"They're moldy," she said, and we threw them out.

Lynne and I each had a box of items we wanted to keep. I had a collection of shot glasses, a horseshoe from the farm, and my books. Lynne took a set of dishes, a gold belt Grandma Jess used to wear, some crystal, and a few surprise items.

Mom kept sneaking things into our boxes. And Lynne got most of the surprises because she made the mistake of staying out of the basement for periods of time and leaving mom and I down there alone

"Do you want this juicer?" she said.

"Does it work?"

"No."

"I don't want it."

"It's a perfectly good juicer. It just needs to be fixed. I think you should take it," my mom said.

"I don't want it," I said.

Mom looked at me. "Lynne would probably want it, don't you think?"

"Yes," I agreed.

"Here, put it in her box."

Then mom would come across a "perfectly good deep fat fryer that needed a little work."

"I don't want it."

"But Lynne will, don't you think?"

"Here, I'll put it in her box," I said.

We worked our way through the stacks and stacks of boxes, Mom fingering things and remembering, Lynne and I hauling ass up and down the stairs. After about trip 26, I found Mom putting safety pins from a drawer one at a time into a jar.

"Mom, what are you doing?" I said.

"These are perfectly good safety pins," she said, holding up the jar.

"You've already got a lifetime supply in that jar," I said. "I think we can pitch the rest."

She looked at me angrily. On the next trip, she was reading through a box of cards.

"Mom," I said.

"You can't throw these cards out. At least not all of them. I'll sort through them and pick out the ones you should keep."

"Mom," I said.

"Oh, pitch them," she said disgustedly. "You have a heart of stone."

By the time we worked our way to the cabinets in the back of the room, we had started drinking Blue Woos. Lynne and I had on matching lampshades, big ones with brown ruffles, and pairs of my great-grandfather's bifocals.

"What's in this toy chest?" Lynne said.

"Open it and see," Mom said.

"Be careful," I said, laughing.

"Why?"

"Remember my gerbils? Remember when Daddy painted the basement, and they got loose? I found one dead in a paint can. Well, I caught the other one, but I couldn't put him back in the cage because it had a hole. And I couldn't let him run around, so I put him in the toy chest. I didn't know he'd suffocate and die."

"RaeAnn," Mom said.

"Is he still in here?" Lynne said, gingerly touching the toy chest lid.

"I don't know."

"Let's not even look," Lynne said. "Let's just carry it up."

"What if something good is in there?" Mom said.

"I'm not touching that box," I said." Let's let Daddy carry it up."

Daddy came downstairs wide-eyed and breathing through his mustache.

"Ray, I'm glad your home. You won't believe what the girls have thrown away. I kept telling them you'd have the big one when you found out, but they just threw it away."

"What, what" he stammered. "What did they pitch?"

"I can't tell you. I'm afraid you'll kill them," she said.

"Daddy, we didn't touch your stuff."

"You should have seen them, Ray. They didn't care what it was—they pitched it all."

"What, what, what?" my dad said, frantically scanning the basement.

"Daddy, don't listen to her," Lynne said.

"Oh, Ray when you find out...."

"You girls better not have touched my race track."

"That was the first to go," mom said.

My dad didn't wait for a response. Instead, he ran upstairs and started rummaging through the junk pile.

"Mom," Lynne said.

"I was just having some fun with him."

Later I called Matt, who had a pickup truck, to help us haul all the stuff to the dump. The four of us, Lynne, Harry, Matt, and I went out drinking. We played darts, and Matt stood close behind me, smelling like whiskey and aftershave. I imagined that he was right behind me, pressing against.

"You're crowding me," I said to him, but he was about three feet away. I don't know if all that dust or all those Blue Woos or feeling him standing behind me made me crazy, but I grabbed Matt and made him dance with me in the middle of the bar to Patsy Cline's "Crazy."

We stumbled in around three a.m., and on my way in, I decided to check on Tilly. I knew that she had been having trouble sleeping lately, and I didn't want to wake her. As I stood outside her door, I thought I heard her call my name.

"RaeAnn," I thought I heard her say, "come here, I want to tell you something." I opened her door and went in.

She was asleep with one arm thrown over her eyes and her mouth hung open. Her sleeping cap was crooked on her head, and her feet peeked out from under the covers. I adjusted her comforter and noticed how skinny her legs had gotten—how whittled down her whole body had become. She looked delicate and fragile like a baby bird. What meat she did have swung from her bones, as if it was barely hanging on. If you cut away all the loose flesh, there'd be nothing left but a skeleton, I thought, a bag of bones.

Tilly hadn't looked this old since when Paw Paw had his stroke and she had let her hair go. Even then, only her face looked tired and old. Now her body looked tired and old.

I sat in the chair by her bed and watched her sleep. When did she get so old? I wondered. Where had all her body slipped away to? I remembered that I used to tickle Tilly's back and rub cream on her. She had strong, meaty arms, and the flesh from her arm hung down like a hammock from below her bone. "Make this fat disappear," she said. I rubbed my magic lotion on it, and Tilly lifted her arm, and to me, it did disappear. Now I wanted to make that muscle come back.

I wondered how she could remain so cheerful in the face of her body going its own way. "At least I got my mind," she would often say. "Ruthie Gilder's mom thinks someone is breaking into her house and stealing the peanut butter. I'd rather lose my body than my mind," she'd told me. "I'm not as old in my head as I look in my body." I compared her to the other old people—those who constantly complained or worse who gave up. How did she put up such a fight?

The next morning Tilly was up dressed in her golf skirt with a fox appliquéd on it and on the matching shirt. She had on her golf socks with the little ball dangling over her tennis shoes, and my mom had removed the toilet paper from around her head and combed her beehive back in place. She smiled as if things were going just her way.

Chapter 11

Promises, Promises

The next morning I heard Daddy talking on the phone and making plans. Then he handed the phone to me. It was Frank.

"Rise and shine, and give God your Glory, glory, Children of the Lord," he sang.

"I'm not talking to you," I said. "You were supposed to help me yesterday."

"Now, RaeAnn," Frank said in his salesman voice. "I've got a good excuse. There was an emergency."

"What kind of emergency?"

"I can't go into the details just yet, but believe me I would have been there to help you if I could have. Now, get your deck shoes on," he said. "We're all going out on your dad's boat."

"Oh no I'm not," I said. "That boat doesn't work."

"Well, I had a friend of mine take a look at it the other day, and I've got it working perfectly. All of us our going out for the day. It's my way to make up for the basement thing," he said.

For some ridiculous reason I agreed, although I hated that boat. My dad had always wanted a boat, and he finally bought a used boat from some guy's driveway on the Southside.

"It's in perfect working order," Daddy claimed. I wasn't so sure, but I helped load up the boat for a trip to Brookville.

"RaeAnn, get the tackle," Frank ordered.

"RaeAnn, load that cooler on," Daddy said.

"RaeAnn, get that big raft out of the trunk," Frank said.

"Count the life jackets, RaeAnn," my dad said. "She's a lifeguard, you know," he said to Frank.

"RaeAnn, did you pack us some sandwiches?"

"RaeAnn, don't forget the brownies."

Finally, we got all the gear loaded in the boat, and then Tilly climbed up the ladder into the boat and we drove to Brookville. With her bad hip, there was no other way Tilly could climb in, so she rode to Brookville, like some bait and tackle beauty queen, waving and looking important from the ski boat.

Next, came the irksome procedure of getting the boat in the water, which my dad could never do without at least four attempts.

"A tad to the right," Frank said. "Looking good."

The boat and the car made an L, with the boat about 25 yards from the water. My dad pulled it out and tried again.

"Easy does it, Ray," Frank coached. "A little to the left."

The car ended up in the ravine on the left side of the ramp, so my dad blew air through his mustache and tried again.

"This time you'll get it. I can feel it," Frank yelled. "Just punch it and head straight into the lake," Frank said, making a lane to the water with his arms. "Straight back," he said pointing and drawing my dad's path with his arms. "Straight back."

The boat went in the ravine on the right side of the ramp.

"Maybe we can lift it in," Frank said.

My dad pulled back one last time and without even looking, drove the boat straight into the water. Tilly clapped.

Next, we piled in with all our respective gear. My dad stood behind the steering wheel of the boat and yelled for everyone to sit down. He pulled out of the dock going about one mile per hour. I could have swam faster than we were going.

We all looked at each other and shrugged. My dad continued at the same snail pace.

"Daddy," I said and stood up.

"Sit down," he said. I sat down.

"Ray, can't we go a little faster," Tilly asked.

My dad blew air through his mustache and moved the throttle a centimeter. The increase in speed was barely noticeable.

"Faster," I yelled.

"Faster," Frank said.

"Faster, faster, faster," we chanted.

My dad looked nervous, but he moved the throttle up a little more. I stood up to ask him if he'd pull me in the raft.

"Sit down," he said.

"Can I ride in this raft behind the boat?" I said crawling along the floor of the boat.

"It's against the law," he said.

"It is not," Tilly said. "Give her a ride."

After a long contemplation, he decided to let me ride in the raft behind the boat. I climbed in and waved them on. He inched across the water. I gave him the thumb's up. He continued to snake along. I gave up. If I'd had a sheet, I could have made a sail and gone faster than he was pulling me. But I was content to be in a raft behind a boat, our boat.

Next, Lynne, very pregnant decided to take a turn on the raft. Daddy snaked her around the lake, and when she went to get back in the boat, she couldn't. We realized we'd left the ladder in the driveway when we loaded Tilly in. We tried to yank her up out of the water and in the boat, but she was too heavy.

"You're a lifeguard. Get in there and give her a push," my dad said and then gave me a little push over the side.

I was supposed to boost Lynne so that Frank and Daddy could yank her in the boat. I swam underneath her, she sat on my head, and I tried to scissor kick her up. She didn't budge. The rescue operation was made worse by the fact that Lynne couldn't stop laughing.

"This isn't going to work," I sputtered.

"Try it again," Frank said.

I let her sit on my head again, but still no movement. Meanwhile, Tilly was laughing so hard that she peed her pants. My dad was blowing air through his mustache, and Frank was drawing Lynne's path with his arms and telling me, "Straight up. Straight up. Straight up."

Finally, I put Lynne back in the raft and from there, she climbed into the boat. Then my dad drove the boat past the NO BOAT buoys into the swimming area, and the boat died. The lifeguards blew their whistles and waved their arms at us. My dad blew air through his mustache and tried to start the boat.

"Swim us out," Frank said.

"She's a lifeguard," my dad said, as I jumped into the water again. He threw me a rope, and while those fat asses sat in the boat, coaching, I held the rope and pulled them out of the no boat area. The waves swarmed me and bashed my legs into the buoys and the boat. I could hear Frank saying, "To the left, RaeAnn.

To the left," drawing my path with his hands.

When we got out of the no boat area, we got a tow, and I didn't say a word to anyone the rest of the day.

Frank didn't call that entire week, and I was glad. He did call the next weekend.

"I'm having a party. Just for you. At my new house," he pitched. "I moved into a house this weekend, and my first party is dedicated to you."

"That doesn't make up for the boating episode," I said.

"Didn't you go to Mass this weekend? Time to forgive and forget. Be merciful as your Father also is merciful. Judge not, and you shall not be judged. Condemn not, and you shall not be condemned. Forgive and you shall be forgiven."

"Still," I started.

"Give and it shall be given unto you. Good measure pressed down and shaken together and running over shall men give unto your bosom. For with the same measure that you mete withal it shall be measured unto you."

"Frank," I said.

"And he told a parable to them. Can the blind lead the blind? Shall they both not fall into the ditch?"

Finally, we were both quiet.

"A cookout. Some volleyball. A few tunes. A keg," he said. "Come on, you can't pass it up."

"When?"

"This Saturday—four o'clock. And can you pick up a couple pounds of hamburger?"

Frank had moved into a house that looked like a bowling alley. The outside was covered with white ceramic tiles. I hated it immediately. In fact, I'm sure that I had never seen an uglier house.

"This is the ugliest house I've ever seen," I said.

"There's my a-number-one girl," Frank said, standing with a group of people in the yard, one of which was Matt. "Yes, she's all mine. Did you bring the hamburger?"

"This is the ugliest house I've ever seen," I said.

"It's a unique, architecturally sound design," Frank said.

"And the rent is cheap," Paulie added. "To clean the outside, all you need is a little Tilex."

Frank escorted me into the kitchen. The floor tiles were warped and threatened to spring from the floor at any second. That morning's or maybe last year's corned beef hash perched on the gas stove. It looked like the stove that Hansel and Gretel were almost cooked in. The oven door didn't have a handle. The refrigerator was huge. I could have climbed in and stood upright. The handle looked like a tire jack. I heaved it open and peered inside. All the shelves had been removed, and the spare keg was inside, chilling.

"How about making some patties?" Frank said.

I nodded. "This is the ugliest house I've ever seen."

It only got worse. The walls to the bathroom were carpeted halfway up the wall.

"Look," I said to Sam. "You don't need a towel. You can just twirl dry against the wall."

You had to climb three steps to get into the shower which was more like a pantry with a garden hose and a shower curtain. The bedrooms were identical: mattresses on the floor, milk crates for shelves, and clothes everywhere.

Although Frank had not taken the time to put away his clothes, he had set up his bulletin board. He had pinned up two pictures of me—one dressed as Mata Hari for a World War II party and one riding in the back of a pickup truck in cutoffs. He had the famous newspaper clipping, or at least a Xerox of the original he carried in his wallet; a picture of his brother who had died in a rappelling accident in North Carolina; a prayer card with St. Jude's prayer; a label from a beer bottle with a phone number on it; and a picture of himself standing against the slate-gray side of a mountain. He didn't have a shirt on, and every muscle in his body looked ready to climb the rest of the mountain. He wore cutoffs and hiking boots with red socks. I had sent him the socks for his birthday. His climbing rope rested in his hand, and a cigarette rested on his lip. The original Marlboro man.

I snooped around in his closet and found a box of letters I

had written him while he was away. I was going to read them, but I heard his loud voice booming in the living room, saying my name.

The living room had a huge map on Montana framed and hung over the legless couch.

"This is where RaeAnn and I are going on our vacation," Frank said. "Backpacking in Montana. One of these days. Isn't that right, RaeAnn."

"My idea of camping is by the pool at the Holiday Inn," I said.

"She loves to camp," he said. "Remember how much fun we had at Brown County?"

The last time we had been camping at Brown County, Frank had some Harley riders use bolt cutters to cut the hinge and take out the back seat of my car. He locked the keys in the car, but "luckily" the trunk was open.

"See they cut this hinge so that you can crawl through the trunk and get the keys," Frank explained. "No big deal."

Then he lost the keys in the lake. Then I had to hike three miles to a phone. Then I got blisters from my new hiking boots because my socks were locked in the car. Then I had to call my dad to bring my keys down. Then the bee on the phone receiver stung my lip, and my lip swelled. Then I started crying and tripped down the trail and tore all the skin off my knees and the palms of my hand. I'd never been camping since.

"RaeAnn loves the outdoor life," Frank was saying. "She's a pretty damn good fisherman, although I taught her everything she knows. Plus her dad has a ski boat that I'm going to fix up."

I wasn't listening. Instead, I watched Matt play volleyball. He leapt up, arms outreached, hit a perfect spike, and landed on his navy blue Chuck Taylor tennis shoes.

"Perfect," I said. Then I saw his little china doll clapping on the sidelines.

"Tilly hasn't been looking too good," I told Frank when I started speaking to him again. "Maybe we could take her out one night this week."

"Sounds good. I'd love to take her for a spin, but this week is out," he said. "Monday night I'm bowling, Tuesday and

Wednesday night I'm filling in for Brian at Connor's, and Thursday night I'm playing in a dart tournament. This weekend me and the boys are going fishing up in Wisconsin. I'll catch a big mess of fish, and we'll have a fish fry for Tilly," he said. "A big fish fry."

"Sure," I said. "Just like you promised—"

He waved me off, and I stopped.

"Okay," I said. "How about next weekend? I told Lynne I would help her finish up the baby's room. We can take Tilly with us. After we help Lynne, we can go to the Moonglow. They've got a nice dart set up."

"I'll be there with bells on," he said.

Chapter 12

Buster Brown's Bride

When my sister Lynne had her first child, Caroline, I was in school in South Carolina. I was away that weekend at my roommate's parent's house. I got a queasy feeling.

"Something is wrong," I told my friend. "Something is wrong."

I tried calling my mother, but there was no answer. My mom and dad weren't home because they were on their way to Lynne's house, and Caroline was born that day.

When Lynne had her second daughter, Nadine, I was in grad school in Maryland. I woke up one morning and told my roommate. "I have to get some cigars. My sister is having a baby today."

"What? How do you know?" she said.

"I just know."

Lynne called that afternoon, and I was prepared, sitting with my cigars and bottle of champagne.

I got another feeling in the middle of that week. Tilly, Mom, and I were at the American Legion. Some lady celebrating her 88th birthday had just keeled over into her pecan pie, and we initially thought she was dead. The paramedics were there, reviving her. She was just drunk.

"I've got a funny feeling," I said. I had had a funny feeling the whole time she was pregnant. "It's Lynne."

"Is she having the baby?" Tilly said, excited.

"I don't know."

We called Daddy, and he said Lynne had just called. She had fallen and broken her ankle, but she was okay. Tilly and I went over that night to help her.

When we got there, she was organizing her wedding pictures. Her leg was in a cast, but she didn't seem too bothered by it.

"Don't you want some help in the baby's room?" I said.

She looked at me as if I were nuts and then asked me to help her get her pictures organized.

"Remember those awful shoes Harry had," she said, looking at a picture from her college days with Harry.

The first time we met Harry, Lynne's husband, he had on ugly, platform shoes. My mom, giver of nicknames, bestowed "Buster Brown" on him and was sure this romance would not amount to anything. Lynne had always been so particular about what her boyfriends wore.

"She'll never marry him with shoes like that," mom said.

Lynne bought him some new shoes and moved in with him. Seeing as how they lived together, my mom couldn't pull the deformity ploy, so she tried other tactics.

"You'll have ugly kids. I'm buying you a case of sunscreen for your honeymoon. Don't go in the ocean with him. Sharks are attracted by white."

Actually Harry didn't turn out too bad. I'd lived with my sister most of her life, and I knew what a trial she could be. I gave him credit just sticking with her. He was a wonderful father, and the two girls were not in the least bit ugly. They were beautiful. Still, my mom wouldn't go in the ocean with him.

Before they got married and moved away, Lynne came home again for a couple months. She and I planned her wedding and spent our days laying at the pool and our nights drinking at the Bulldog. That was when our house caught on fire.

Our house caught on fire twice. The first time, my dad was cleaning paintbrushes down the basement with turpentine. He stopped to pee, decided to light up a cigarette, and kaplooey.

My mom hurried us out of the house. I was crying for my gerbils, our Bulldog was hunching some dog down the street, and my mom was asking my dad, "Are you okay? Are you hurt?"

"Uh," he said. "I got burnt."

"Where?"

He blew air through his mustache. "Down there."

He never did tell the fireman when they asked if he was

burnt, although I guess he did have to explain to the doctor.

On the eve of the second fire, I was spending the night at Carla Pentaski's house. Daddy and Aunt Kay's second husband went fishing for the weekend, so Aunt Kay and the boys stayed with Mom. Mom, Aunt Kay, and Lynne ordered pizza with hot peppers, drank beer, and smoked cigarettes, talking about Lynne getting married. Kay dropped a cigarette in my dad's chair. She pulled it out with the fire still on the tip, and Mom poured beer down the chair and said, "It's out."

They went to bed. Meanwhile, the chair started to smolder. Like my dad, the chair, a big, red, plush chair with an ottoman, sat in front of the TV and smoked all night.

Lynne smelled the smoke and climbed out my window with the two boys. Mom tried to put the fire out with a pan of water, running back and forth from the chair to the kitchen with a saucepan. Aunt Kay woke up and, with all the smoke, couldn't see and thought she had gone blind, like Blind Billy, our cousin blind from moonshine. She tried to make her way to the door, knocked the TV off the dresser, tumbled down the stairs like a stunt woman, crashed through the wrought iron hanging on the landing, and landed on the hutch. She ran to the next-door neighbor's, threw a rock the window, and jumped up and down in the street until the firemen got there.

The firemen put out the fire and rescued Lynne, who descended from the roof in her nightie, while the firemen crowded around the bottom of the ladder.

The fire damage wasn't bad, but smoke invaded every crook and cranny in our house. We had to take all our clothes to the cleaners and stay at a hotel. During our stay at the hotel, Paw Paw died, and we all had to borrow clothes to wear to the funeral because ours were being de-smoked at the cleaners.

For about two months, we didn't have any furniture or carpet in our house. My Doberman had eaten the three piece sectional we had, so that took care of the couch. The chair had set itself in flames, and the workers tore up the carpet and painted all the closets. We sat in lawn chairs on the bare-board floor and argued over the color of carpet we should get. And we tried to plan Lynne's wedding in the midst of this mess.

The impending wedding and the thought of his upright Lutheran family meeting our motley crew gave Lynne a case of nerves so bad that patches of her hair fell out. Luckily the veil covered it. It was actually during this time that Aunt Kay and Mom planned to ask Harry's father, who was very short, to see whether he could walk under Mom's outstretched arm although they didn't actually do it until years later.

The wedding fireworks started the night before the rehearsal. The day of the rehearsal my dad came running in our room.

"Lynne, Lynne, Lynne," he chanted in his Hanes underwear.

Lynne opened her eyes, looked at him, and rolled over.

"Ignore him," I said. "It's just a bad dream."

"Lynne, Lynne" he said.

"Better answer him, or he'll stand there all day," I said.

"Lynne, Lynne—."

"What?" she said.

"You don't have to yell at me."

"What do you want?" she asked.

"Let me see," he said. "I forget now. Oh yeah, your car's been stolen. Your car's not out front. It's been stolen. Your car has been stolen."

I started to giggle, and Lynne rolled over.

"Go ask your wife where my car is," she said. Mom and Tilly had decided to have their own bachelorette party, so they ventured out in Harry's car, nicknamed the Boat because you had to rotate the wheel three times to turn a corner. The Boat was a '72 light blue Ford. The trunk held three kegs. You didn't need a key to start the car. You just turned the ignition.

Mom and Tilly set out without a key to the Alley Cat Lounge to have a few beers. When they got ready to come home, they realized they had locked the doors, so Tilly stood in the middle of the road and flagged down a policeman. Somehow they explained how they didn't have a key, how their daughter/granddaughter was getting married, how they needed a ride home, and so on. Lynne and I arrived home just in time to see the police car pull into our driveway. Tilly's beehive was barely visible above the dashboard in the front seat. She got out of the car grinning.

In fact, she laughed so hard on the way into the house that she fell in the bushes. She lay there laughing and pointing at us, her new perspective on things only adding to the hilarity of the occasion. The more we tugged to get her out, the harder she laughed and the heavier she got. We finally had to get a neighbor to help us hoist her out of the bushes.

The rehearsal went great, except for Daddy. Daddy wore his glasses upside down, drank rusty nails, played a song with his crystal wine glass, and sang his fraternity sweetheart song to my mom during dinner. He couldn't help it—he was nervous.

Since the engagement, my dad had walked around the house, breathing through his mustache and reciting, rehearsing, practicing his one line. When the priest said, "Who gives this bride away?" Daddy got to say, "Her mother and I do." For eight months, we could hear him somewhere in the house testing out intonations, stressing different syllables, enunciating the five words in his one line: "Her mother and I do."

The morning of the wedding Mom, Tilly and Lynne went to the beauty parlor, and I stayed home with Daddy. As I was curling my hair in the bathroom, I heard the familiar line and turned around. My dad stood there in his underwear, undershirt, black socks and rented tux shoes. Grinning. I grinned back. Next he was back with the pants to his tux on. Not the pants and the shoes, just the pants. He returned every couple of minutes with each piece of his ensemble on until finally he was standing there in his underwear and undershirt with the bow tie clipped to his new undershirt.

"Her mother and I do," he said.

When the time came for him to recite his famous line, he forgot it. To give him credit, it was confusing. The priest in rehearsal did not say he would give a short prayer over the three of them before the fated question. During the prayer my dad started to back away and then inched forward. He looked as if he might just blurt his one line out in the middle of the prayer. Finally, the priest intoned, "Who gives this bride away?"

"Oh," my dad stammered and blew air through his mustache. "I, hmm... " he said.

My aunt and I started to laugh.

"Um, well," he said. Finally he gave up. "Me." He beamed and sat down.

My dad wasn't the only one who embarrassed himself. My aunt got her dress caught in her shoe and tripped down the aisle. "Damn shoe," I heard her say. And Tilly before the night was over would take another spill in the restroom.

Harry's poor family didn't know what they were in for. Harry's mother, Ella did not drink.

"Can I get you a beer, Rosie?" Tilly said.

"Her name is Ella," I said.

"She looks more like a Rosie to me," Tilly said.

"I don't drink," Ella said.

"You should," Tilly said. "Beers got calcium. Good for your bones. That's the only reason I drink it," Tilly said sipping her beer.

My mother was at this time parading around with my sister's veil on, my uncle was dancing the tango with a bridesmaid, and my dad was by the keg telling jokes. Lynne was making the rounds, Harry was grinning. About halfway through the reception, Harry's aunt came and got me.

"It's your grandmother," she said.

I followed her in the restroom and heard Tilly's voice. "All I can see is that damn green dress. Get that damn green dress out of my way."

She was sitting on the middle of the floor with her beer. Ella, in her green dress, was trying to help her up.

"Look, RaeAnn," Tilly said. "I didn't spill a drop of my beer."

With Aunt Kay's help, I hoisted her up and muttered some apology. Later Aunt Kay tripped again over her shoes and dropped three Swedish meatballs in Harry's Aunt Primrose's lap. Even I added to the family's reputation by standing on a table and singing, "Hambone, hambone have you heard/ Pappa's gonna buy you a mocking bird," baring my whole leg to slap the beat.

Harry and Lynne finally left for the honeymoon, and we all made it home. The next day the accusations started to fly.

"Who told Harry's father the joke about the Lutheran

minister?" my mom said.

"I didn't know they were Lutheran," Daddy said.

"Who wearing the veil and saying over and over she never got a real wedding?" Aunt Kay said.

"Who tripped...?"

"Who danced....?"

"Who fell....?"

"Where is Tilly?" I said.

"I'm in here with the wedding gifts," Tilly called from the next room.

She sat between two stacks of presents: ones she had figured out by shaking, feeling, rattling, and ones she had yet to determine the contents.

"I can't figure this one out," she said. "I've got all these."

My dad picked up a present from the "known" pile. "What's this?"

"Crock pot."

"This?" Aunt Kay said.

"Bath towels."

"This?"

"Serving platter for meat."

"How can you tell that?" I said.

"Push the box in. You can feel the outline," she said.

I tried it. "Serving platter for meat."

"Help me with this one. I can't figure it out."

We each took turns shaking the box, offering suggestions, deciding it couldn't be that until finally Tilly turned innocently to Daddy, "Ray, where's your pen knife?"

"No," my mom said. "We can't."

"They won't be back for a whole week," Tilly said.

"We shouldn't," Aunt Kay said.

"RaeAnn could open it with the knife, and no one would ever know," Tilly said. My dad handed me the knife.

I opened it and peeked inside. "Guess," I said.

"RaeAnn," they screamed in unison.

I opened the box, took out one of the items, and held it up for them to see.

"Corn-on-the-cob holders. A dozen of them."

They groaned.

"Figures Claire would get something cheap like that, even though they could spend fifty thousand dollars to join that country club in Wakarusa," my mom said. We groaned again.

After the honeymoon, Lynne and Harry came back to the house to open the presents. "Open this one first," I said and handed her the corn-on-the-cob holders. We laughed when she opened them, and Lynne and Harry though we were laughing at the absurdity of the gift.

"Open that one next," Tilly said and pointed to the serving platter. "I can't imagine what it could be."

Lynne opened it and held it up. "It's a serving platter for meat," she said.

"Who would have guessed?" Tilly said.

After they opened the presents, Lynne asked me, "Are you packed? I want you to come stay with me for a couple days, a week, to help me organize my house. You can sleep in the extra bedroom."

"She's not going with you," mom said. "You've only been married a week."

"She's my sister, and I want her to come home with me."

"No definitely not."

She looked at Tilly, but Tilly didn't say anything. Instead I stayed home, and Lynne cried when she left and said next week I was coming regardless of what mom said and that I was staying all week.

"You're my sister," she said to me.

When Lynne left, I cried too, and mom came in and hugged me. "She'll always be your sister," she said. "Don't cry."

Lynne and I have shared a lifetime. Being put to bed early. Taking baths together and coaxing the dog to jump in with us. Whispering late at night while car lights whirled bright visions around our room. Playing our 45's and dancing on the bed. Making pies from sawdust, mulberries and shaving cream. We put one in the refrigerator, and Daddy, who was babysitting, saw it and took not one, but two bites from it. "I knew it tasted funny," he said. "But it looked so good."

We shared not only the same bedroom, but the same

childhood. Raised on the same myths, we had cringed at the same voice beckoning, "Get down here this instant," delighted at "Wait at the top of the steps while Daddy checks to see if Santa Claus came," and held the same truths to be self-evident, "Shoes on the bed, bad luck."

After Lynn and I looked through all her pictures, reminiscing, we both laid together on the pull-out couch in the living room.
"Remember decorating Mahoney's basement."
"We made it into a dungeon."
"And you got stuck in their tree. Mom had forbid you to climb it."
"And you got me down by letting me sit on your head."
"We both fell."
"Remember walking Falstaff to the ice cream store." Falstaff was our English bulldog.
"He'd run all the way down there, eat his ice cream cone, and walk to the phone booth."
"He wouldn't budge from that phone booth."
"We'd have to call Daddy to come pick us up."
"He was a smart dog."
"Remember when we went on vacation and you sent him a postcard at the kennel."
"I did?"
"The lady said he sniffed it and went crazy."
"Remember roller skating down the basement."
"Love grows where my Rosemary goes and nobody knows but me," we sang.
"Hey, I've got our old 45's," Lynne said.
"Let's get them out."
We got them out and played our old favorites, *Mony Mony*, *Judy in Disguise*, *Itsy Bitsy Teeny Weeny Yellow Polka Dot Bikini*. When Harry came home from work, he found us bouncing on the bed singing into candlesticks. He just shrugged and said "Sisters."

Chapter 13

Sisters

We barely made it home from our mid-week trip, when Lynne called again. "It's time," she said.

We had a running pool going on her newest baby—date of birth, sex, and weight. When Lynne called, I grabbed the baby scorecard, and Tilly, Daddy, Mom, and I piled into the van at one a.m. and headed toward Illinois.

"Hurry, hurry, hurry," Daddy said, corralling us into the van. "Hurry, hurry, hurry. We're going to miss it."

He had his stopwatch around his neck, and he blew air through his mustache as he packed the van. Inside the van, with the trolling motor from his boat, his tackle box, four suitcases, three pillows, and two coolers, there was barely room for our bodies. Tilly and I scrunched in the back. She had on her lampshade cap and her robe. I had on a sweatshirt and my hair tied in a bandanna. We tried to think of names for the baby as Daddy headed towards the highway.

"How about Loretta?" Tilly said.

"How about Herbie?" my dad said.

"How about Matt?" I said.

Daddy and Mom smoked like fiends on the way over, especially after we ran out of gas. Luckily, we ran out a block before the interstate, right near a gas station.

"My daughter is having a baby," he told the attendant.

The attendant looked at me, and Tilly laughed.

When we finally made it over to Lynne's house, and she was sitting at the kitchen table and shuffling cards.

"Want to play some euchre?" she said.

"I thought I was going to miss it," my dad said.

"Let's play some cards," Tilly said. Tilly played as Lynne's partner, and Daddy and I teamed up. We beat them the first round ten to four.

"Good God, kid, did you forget how to play?" Tilly said to

Lynne when she didn't call trump on a potential hand.

"Don't yell at a pregnant woman," Lynne said.

" If you keep playing like this, you'll be going to the hospital one way or another." It was Tilly's deal, and because her arm was shaky, she usually had me deal for her. "I'll deal them myself," she said and yanked the cards from me. Then she called hearts alone and took all the tricks.

"See how simple that was," she said to Lynne. "That's how you play. I like to play as RaeAnn's partner because she's reckless. She'll call it on anything."

Tilly and Lynne beat us the second round ten to nothing.

"I smell something nasty in here," Tilly said. "I think it's a skunk."

During the third, the rubber game of the match, Lynne said, "I think it's time."

We woke Harry up, and Lynne, Harry, and I piled in Lynne's van to go to the hospital. I had decided to be a witness to the birthing process this time around. Tilly laughed so hard that she couldn't talk.

"As sick as you get at the sight of blood? I hope they have a room next door for you," Tilly said, in between fits of hysteria.

"One so that they can tie up her tubes," Mom said.

"I'll be okay."

"You know the baby's head has to come through that little hole," Tilly said, and then she threw her head back and really laughed.

"I know how a baby is born," I said.

Because this was her third child, we all expected Lynne to go quick. On the way to the hospital, Harry stopped at the post office to mail some letters. I thought we were there and wondered why a hospital had so many mail boxes in front. Then he stopped at the bank and made a deposit; again, I reached for the door although the drive-through windows did catch my eye. He pulled out of the bank, and I wondered if we'd every get there. I was ready to carry Lynne piggyback to the hospital to get there.

When we finally arrived, they took Lynne to the birthing room. It looked like a room at the Chat and Rest Hotel: yellow striped wallpaper, a three-D picture of an owl, and a macramé hanging with a little canary perched inside. A tape recorder sat next to the bed. I wondered what you'd make a tape of—a tape of you screaming your head off, or maybe a play-by-play. A TV was suspended over the birthing bed. I expected stainless steel and nurses and doctors milling around in their scrubs. Instead, I was in a low rent Ho-Jo's with one nurse half asleep in the hallway. But, indeed, she had the baby in that very room.

The nurse hooked Lynne up to a monitor that kept track of her contractions and the baby's heart beat. It made sounds like a whale belching on a Jacques Cousteau special. The constant burp burp burp made me edgy. I had been edgy the whole time she was pregnant—maybe because I knew that I was going to witness the birth or maybe because that death trifecta was hanging around my mind.

Finally, at six a.m., the nurse sent me home. At the time, my sister's Doberman count was at eight. I came home, and not one of them barked. As I snuck upstairs, I noticed one staring at me. No wonder they don't bark. They were going to let me get in and then take me apart, limb by limb.

"Max, it's me. It's me Max." The dog didn't move.

My mom woke up and screamed when she saw me standing at the end of the bed talking to the dog. I gave her the baby update.

"Will Lynne be okay?" I said.

"Yes, now be quiet before you wake up all the other dogs."

Around one o'clock the next afternoon, Harry called and told me to come on if I wanted to watch. When I got there Lynne was sweating and having some wicked contractions that racked her body. She had Harry hold her up and she'd grab his hair and pull it as hard as she could each time she had a contraction. The nurse calmly came in and checked her every so often. Then she finally said it was time.

We got suited up, and the doctor came in with a big cart of steel instruments, and they made the bed into a birthing chair. Later, on the way home, my dad said the doctor is more like a centerfielder. "Take two steps back and make the catch," he said.

Lynne was really having some contractions now.

"Can you see okay?" the doctor said.

"I can see plenty," I said.

Finally, Lynne let loose two, 20 second screams, and then the baby came flying out, all bloody and beautiful. I started crying when I saw her.

The only thing I remembered clearly was seeing that it was a girl. I also remembered the needle the doctor used for some shot during the process was as long as my forearm. I almost passed out when I saw it. Then when he gave her an episeotomy and stitched her up, I didn't want to look, but I accidentally saw what I imagined to be a big sewing needle and some cat-gut thread. That really set me shaking. Plus the after birth didn't come out all the way, so the doctor had to fish around for it with some plier-like looking tool. Then he held it up for me to see.

But the baby was beautiful. She was tiny, just 6 pounds, and didn't cry except for one second. She had smooth pretty skin and lots of hair that stood at attention like a crew cut my dad once had. She was curious and looked as if to say, "Who the hell are you?" They named her Jessica after my grandmother.

Mom, Tilly, Daddy, and the girls came up to the hospital to see the baby. The girls were ecstatic that it was a baby girl.

"She's beautiful, isn't she," I said to Caroline.

"Yes, but not as pretty as me," she said.

"You won't be the baby anymore," I said to Nadine. She looked at me like she hated me.

Afterward, Tilly, the girls, Mom and I went to the store, and immediately Nadine started screaming her head off for animal crackers. Mom tried to quiet her by putting her hand over her mouth.

"Why don't you tell her to `cry harder?'" I said.

"Not in public," Tilly said.

"Oh, I forgot," I said. "In public, you get the old `If I have to pull your pants down here in public and crack you on the ass, I will.'"

"Here Nadine," Mom said. "I've got the cookies."

She placed them in the cart, and Nadine started screaming even louder. Mom put her hand over her mouth again. She started wailing and kicking her feet. You could hear her throughout the store.

"Child Abuse. Aisle seven," I said as if I were talking over the PA.

My mom didn't think that was very funny. Then Caroline and Nadine got in a fight over who got to ride in the cart.

"Let Nadine," I said. "She's the youngest."

"Ohhhh," Carolyn grunted and stomped her feet. "I hate her. I like my new sister, but I hate Nadine."

"Listen," I said. "Don't say that. She's your sister, and you love her."

Caroline glared at me.

"You know your mother and I are sisters, and when we were little, we used to fight, too. But we always loved each other."

"Mom's sister?" Nadine asked.

"Just like you're Caroline's sister," I said.

They both threw their heads back and laughed at the thought. Later we stopped at McDonald's and ordered two Happy Meals, but got a Happy Meal and a fish sandwich instead.

"I swear they put the idiots at the drive-through because they know you can't get at them," Mom said.

The girls fought over the one Happy Meal until we turned around and got a second one. Then they fought over who got the new Happy Meal. We finally made it home with the two girls in tow. Tilly poured a glass of straight vodka. Mom and I stared. She took off her diamond rings and dropped them in.

"It cleans them," she said.

Mom took the bottle from her and poured a glass and drank it. Daddy snored in front of the TV. Nadine was trying to ride one of the eight Dobermans around the house, and Caroline sat at my feet painting my toenails pink.

"I'm too old for this," Mom said.

"It's just beginning," Tilly said. "You'll like being a grandmother."

"RaeAnn," Caroline asked me, "if I pick my nose will my hair fall out?"

"Yes," I said without thinking. Then I realized that the indoctrination of Lynne's girls had begun.

Harry's parents came over that night and because Lynne was not there to ensure our place of position in the house, we were moved to the motor home. Daddy, Tilly, Mom, and I all slept together, like one big happy family. Set on a slant, Mom had to run up the aisle and leap into her bed. Every time she rolled over, she fell out. Tilly was propped in her bed with her wedding-rice cap perched on her head. She was drinking crème de menthe. I was smoking a cigar.

"What's it like having a baby?" I said.

"It's the most wonderful experience of your life," my mom said.

"It's like shitting a bowling ball," Tilly said. "It's like shitting a telephone pole."

My mom and Tilly stayed with Lynne, and my dad drove me home. We stopped by the hospital to see the baby one last time, but the nurses were giving the baby a bath.

"Do you want me to go get her?" the nurse said.

"No, I'll be seeing her plenty," I said.

On the way home, Daddy and I drank beers and smoked cigars.

"I remember when Lynne was born. Your mom fixed me some soup. I got a can opener and sat down to eat it. Then I got some towels and some ink to take with us. The towels were for if her water broke, the ink for announcements. I don't know what I was thinking.

"I had a class that afternoon, so I stopped to see my teacher. `Mr. Stump,' I said. `I won't be in class this afternoon.' He asked me why. I said, `My wife's having a baby.' He said, `Get outta here, Ray.'

"I took your mom to the hospital, but back then, they didn't let anyone in so I sat in the waiting room and smoked about a pack of cigarettes. When she did have the baby, I was in the bathroom. They had to page me."

"And she was an ugly baby right?" I said.

"Oh, no, she was beautiful, just tiny, like a little bird. You, on the other hand, were a big, healthy baby. You looked like a big doll, and one side of your head was flat."

I frowned and felt the side of my head. "I didn't know my head was flat."

"Yep, flat like a pancake."

My dad and I rode a couple minutes in silence, and then he looked at me and grinned.

"I'm the happiest man alive," he said.

When we got home, I called Frank.

"It's a girl," I said.

"When are you coming home? I've got some big plans for us this weekend."

"She's beautiful," I said.

"Too bad it wasn't a boy."

"What did you say?"

"Too bad it wasn't a boy. I'd be disappointed if I had all girls."

"He should be lucky the baby was healthy," I said raising my voice. "Besides, what's the matter with all girls. My dad has two girls and never regretted it."

"I bet if you asked him, he'd say he really always wanted a boy."

"I don't have to ask him," I said. "I know. I've known all my life. He has never been disappointed with Lynne and I. He's never wished we were boys. Never made us feel bad for being girls. Never."

"Calm down," Frank said.

That night, instead of calling Frank like I was supposed to, I went to the Bulldog. Matt was there, sans his china doll, and we played darts.

"Another girl," he said. "Harry's a lucky guy, probably the happiest man alive right now."

I surprised him by kissing him on the cheek and by kicking his ass at darts.

117

Chapter 14

Earache's Bride

The wedding of Eric and Emma was looming closer, and I still hadn't rigged up a date. I knew that it'd take some finagling to get Frank to take me.

"Listen to this," Frank said. "I learned a new song on my guitar." He started to play "Dixie Chicken."

"Will you take me to Emma's wedding this Saturday?" I blurted.

"You know weddings aren't my style."

I sat in silence.

"But, for you, I'll think about it."

Normally, I would have planned a better strategy to get him to take me, but I only had a few days until the wedding, and I couldn't go to Emma's wedding without some sort of escort.

The impending wedding of Emma greatly depressed me. Of all people, she needed to marry a doctor. In high school, we kept a medical chart on Emma taped to our locker door. In gym, while we sweated, running around the track, and the boys in study hall in the library bet on us like racehorses, Emma sat in the shade.

"I have asthma," she said.

She said she ruptured a membrane in her nose because she blew her nose the wrong way. She read about it in *Glamour*. She told us her vagina just wasn't the same since she slept in a tampon.

Her medical chart for one month read like this: February 1st, a toothache; the 2nd, a splinter the size of a two-by-four; the 3rd, she coughed and said something came flying out of her mouth. On the 4th, she was going bald; on the 5th, she had a sore throat; on the 6th, she gave a pint of blood.

"You only have eight pints, and it takes a while to get it back. Besides, I may be anemic."

The 8th, she got food poisoning from the microwave ham

sandwich she had for lunch. The 10th, she had so much mucous in her esophagus she couldn't' swallow. She felt awful on the 12th. On the 14th, she had a touch of the flu; the 15th, she had the flu; and on the 16th, she had an ulcer.

On the 17th she didn't know if she was sick from cramps, from working out, or from her uniform being too tight. She was sick from junk food on the 18th. The next day the left side of her brain was not functioning. On the 20th, she told us she was giving up complaining for Lent, but as she said it, she coughed and strained a muscle in her abdomen. On the 21st, she said "shit was coming out of my eyeball."

The next day, she wanted to see "the violent cell wars going on in my body." The 23rd she was in pain, and on the 25th she confessed that she saw *Ben Hur* and thought she had "leopard-cee."

"Don't forget," Sam said, "I gave you lead poisoning in fourth grade."

We often wondered why we were even friends with Emma, but we were. We liked Emma because she was gullible. She lent herself to practical jokes because she took herself so seriously. Next to her senior picture, a double-silhouette portrait done by a special studio, Emma wrote, "I want to star on Broadway, be called the next Marilyn Monroe, and make a movie of my life." Next to Sam's it said, "I want to graduate."

In grade school, Emma had beautiful blond hair that her mom rolled every night in perfect ringlets cascading down her back. Emma always moved stiffly, afraid if she moved too suddenly a curl would fall out of place. At the time I was swimming competitively and barely had enough hair to shove into two pigtails. I was a constant victim of static electricity, and Sam had a pixie.

Emma always wore frilly, lacy dresses with matching bows tied in her hair. The bows made her look as if her ponytail had sprouted wings and were about to fly away. While we raced around the playground playing Batman and Robin, while we swung upside down from the bike racks, while we played four square, jacks, kickball, Emma sat on the steps, reading (or pretending to read) a book. The nuns chided us for ripping our uniforms, for looking unruly, for running. They praised Emma for her neatness.

"Such a sweet studious girl," they said. "Did you see, she's reading *Joseph and His Coat of Many Colors* today."

At Billy Martin's party Sam spilt punch on Emma's pink dress. At eighth grade graduation, Sam accidentally stepped on the back of Emma's dress and ripped it. In high school, Sam gave Dave Frederickson the combination to her locker, and he put a snake in it. Sam taped a blown up French Tickler purchased from the bathroom at the Alley Cat on her locker. Sam told Emma that she was probably pregnant because she saw Pete Hanover jack off in the swimming pool right next to her.

"Sperm can swim, you know," she said.

"Oh my God," Emma cried and pushed her hands to her belly.

When Emma expressed surprise that you could have sex when you are pregnant, Sam told her, "Why do you think babies have a soft spot?"

We probably would have felt guiltier about some of the things we did to Emma, but she gloated about everything—her career as freshman cheerleader, her capped teeth, and her Adonis among mortal men, the doctor. I knew I had to go to both her bridal shower and her wedding, and I was dreading it.

Sam and I went to the shower together, first stopping at the Bulldog to fortify ourselves for the occasion.

"I'll never get married," I lamented.

"Good. I'll be damned if I'll let you ruin your life." Sam took a swig of her beer and announced loudly, "I have the mating habits of a penguin."

I laughed.

"What are the mating habits of a penguin, and how do you know what they are?"

"Once a year. And I know because I live it."

"And when we do have sex," Sam said, "the theme to 'Rawhide' keeps running through my head. Head 'em up, move 'em out, move 'em out, head 'em up, R—A—W—H—I—D—E."

Three guys playing darts laughed. Encouraged, Sam

continued.

"I spend Saturday nights reading smut novels and flipping through the men's underwear section of the Sear's catalog. There's quite a few boners," she said to one of the laughing dart players. "See page seventy-eight."

"Sam!".

"I'm not joking," Sam said. "It was different before I got married. Then," she said loudly, "then he could have gotten it up for a napkin ring."

"Like my mom says, the minute they say I do, it becomes I used to," I said.

"Anyway, you adore Shreve.".

"Sure I do. That's what makes it so awful," Sam said. "The thing that really pisses me off is that I'd decided to start charging him for it, you know, fifty bucks a pop. I planned on making enough money to buy a new living room set from Sears, you know, the couch, loveseat, chair, ottoman, the works. Tilly gave me the idea. But now, now, he doesn't even want it."

We left the Bulldog and headed for the bridal shower. The shower was what we expected.

"I hope this baby is as wonderful as my Jason," Sally said. "Why, Jason is a perfect child."

"Jason should be locked in a dog cage," Sam said to me. "He goes to the same day care center as Thomas."

"The teachers, everyone just loves him," Sally said. "He's so sweet and precious."

"When is the new baby due?" Trixie said.

"September," she said. "It's going to be a girl because I dreamt about pink bows the night I conceived her. A matched set."

Sally and her husband took this baby business seriously— taking the temperature to determine when she was ovulating, planning to deliver in time to take the kid off for tax purposes, and so on. Sally told me when they had Jason and were determining ovulation, her husband thought you took a vaginal temperature.

"Whoa. Hundred and eight. You're ready, honey," Sam said.

Jason, alias the Christ Child, was bald as a bowling bowl, save his eyebrows. He had a uni-brow, one bushy eyebrow extending from one temple to the next. He looked to me like a Dr. Seuss character (the Grinch who stole Christmas, I think), like he had a fur-trimmed cap pulled down over his head.

"I dreamt that when Thomas was born he had thirteen teeth," Sam said.

A premonition, I noted. For when his teeth did come in, they were big as playing cards. I have a picture of him in the front row at a day care pageant, smiling with those playing-card teeth.

"How is Thomas?" Sally asked. "Jason thinks he is so, well, so unique. Of course, they won't be together long. Jason will be in Advanced Kindergarten. He's just so smart."

"Yes, I recall his teacher saying he was the smart-ass of the class," Sam replied, saying smart-ass so that Sally couldn't be sure if she'd said smart-ass or smartest.

"I saw our paper boy masturbating last week on our street. I didn't know whether to call the police or invite him in for waffles," Mary-Lynne said. Her second husband had some kind of cancer and although he could have sex, he couldn't ejaculate. She always worked this topic into the conversation somehow.

"How are things?" Sam said to her.

"Still the same. The doctor is looking into some additional treatments. Of course, even if they do work, I won't be able to have any more kids."

"Do you want anymore?" Trixie said.

"With the state of the world and the possibilities of his cancer being cured, I don't think so."

"I'd hate to be a kid right now. See your friends on grocery bags," I said, since I couldn't think of anything else.

"Did you meet Emma's mother-in-law?" Trixie said. "I hear she's a real bear. No one good enough for her son, the *doctor*."

"Definitely the type to come over and do the white glove test," I said.

"Shreve's mom always sniffs our bedroom when she comes over."

"She does not," I said.

"I caught her in the bedroom last time they were over, but I didn't actually hear any sniffing."

I maintained my composure through the shower, but next I had the wedding to face. Finally, Frank said he would go.
"Okay, okay," he said. "But I'll have to borrow your dad's shoes."
On the day of the wedding, I got all dolled up, shined my dad's wing tips, and sat by the window. My mom grinned.
"What are you laughing at?"
"Remember the Indy 500?"
"Damn it," I said. "He better not."
"Frank wouldn't do that," Tilly said.
"He'll be here. He promised," I said.
"I'd call someone else to get a ride before they leave," Mom said.
I finally called Frank, and his mom said he had gone fishing. I called Sam, Trixie, and everyone else I knew that was going, but everyone was already gone.
"Call Matt," Tilly said.
"I'm not going with him and the China Doll."
"Would you rather go by yourself?"
I called Matt, and he came and got me. I was too frazzled to realize the China Doll was absent.
Emma's wedding of course had to be the biggest and most elaborate. Limos were rented. Flowers, bridesmaids' dresses and shoes were all dyed the same color. A special train was added to her mother's wedding gown. "It's eight feet long and the pearls were sewn on by hand," she'd said. The newest hotel was secured for the reception, and the prettiest cathedral in Indianapolis for the wedding. "Did you see my engagement ring," she'd said at the shower. "It's a special stone cut especially for me."
"You are so beautiful," echoed through the cathedral as she strolled down the aisle. After "You Are So Beautiful" played, we heard "My Eyes Adored You," and then the ceremony started. As Eric knelt on the altar, we saw HELP ME written in bright pink fingernail polish on the heels of his shoes.

"The polish at least matches the bridesmaids' dresses," Trixie said.

I peered around to see who was there. All the girls we had grown up with were there with their husbands. The first one I spotted was Janie Inola.

She netted her husband at the boat, sport, and travel show. She invested $100: $80 in tanning booth sessions, $10 in printed raffle tickets, and $10 in tackle. In the middle of winter, she donned her bikini (she had the tan and the body to do it) and went to the show at the fairgrounds. She walked around, said she was a representative of Captain Hook's Boats, and selectively passed out raffle tickets to win the 20-foot BassMaster displayed in the center coliseum.

Then when she had collected the names and addresses of the prospects she deemed possibilities, she called her first line on the phone and said although he hadn't won the boat, he had won win some free tackle. She arranged to meet him and reeled in the first one. He got $10 in tackle, and she got a two-carat diamond.

Even Louise Barr, who had the worst bucked teeth you'd ever seen, had a man. Her teeth protruded at a 45 degree angle over her lip. They weren't so much bucked as bent. She wasn't the brightest student. When we were studying World War II, she put down Catherine the Great for 5 out of 7 of the fill-in the blank questions. When she heard Ronald Reagan had a polyp, she thought he had a pile-up. "Well, it's up in his ass, isn't it," she said. Louise knocked herself out in gym class by dropping a dumbbell on her own head. Louise once wore her bra backwards all day because she put it on that way, and thought it was bad luck to change it. She married a car mechanic and moved to Tennessee. I can see her waving in the back of that red Isuzu brat, pregnant, leaving for her honeymoon in the Pocono's. "The bathtub is heart-shaped," she screamed. We were happy for her because she had achieved her dream, to stay in a hotel with a heart-shaped bathtub.

Sweet Polly Purebred was there with Gary Oswillier. Becky (her real name) had screwed every lineman on the football team, had mooned every driver she passed on Saturday nights, and had jumped out of Jimmy McMichael's bachelor party cake and let

Skip Johnson lick icing from her thighs. But now Becky was innocent and pure as the Virgin Mary. She collected recipes, wore an apron with a big cherry appliquéd on the front, and quit drinking and smoking because "Gary didn't like it." Becky had once dated Sam's husband, and when we were at a party in Muncie, Sam said, "That girl looks like Becky."

"It's not her," I said.

"It looks like her," Sam said and walked over and kicked her in the shins as hard as she could.

Ethel Miller was there without her husband. He was probably out on some big case—her husband was a dog catcher. The first time I met him, he was flipping through a book with dogs on the cover, and he held it up and gave me a significant look.

"Do you have a dog?" I asked.

"Nooooo," he said.

I waited for an explanation, but seeing as how he didn't offer one, I asked, "Are you thinking about buying a dog?"

"Noooooo," he said and smirked like I was an idiot. I felt like I was on "What's My Line?"

"Do you like dogs?" he said.

"Noooo," he replied.

I finally gave up and asked Ethel what he had the dog book for.

"He's a dog catcher," she said.

I almost bit a hole through my tongue. I thought dogcatchers only existed in comic strips.

"He used to be a security cop, and he worked part-time as a dogcatcher," she explained. "Now he's devoted himself to dog catching."

I nodded.

"Guess what," she said, "he used to only be able to write out a ticket for a maximum of thirty dollars when he was a security cop, but yesterday he wrote out fines totaling three hundred dollars. To one person. Imagine that!"

The next time I saw the dogcatcher, he had little evidence bags with little piles of shit all bagged up, taped and neatly marked with a pen. He had snapshots of battered dogs he showed me.

Still, Ethel got to trot down the aisle. I smiled at all of my married friends and dreaded the ever-looming question, "Are you seeing anyone?"

As we filed out of church, Ethel came barreling towards me in her red polka-dotted dress, looking like a case of measles bearing down on you. She grabbed my arm.

"I didn't know you were dating Matt Tyler," she whispered. "Imagine that."

Matt smiled.

The reception was grand. Melons sculptured into swans, embossed napkins, finger sandwiches, platters of shrimp, Swedish meatballs and other delicacies, platters of perfectly rolled and aligned lunchmeats, waiters at the door with champagne.

"Think this is Eckrich bologna?" Sam said.

We piled our plates, found a table, and surveyed the crowd. The men hung out around the keg, and the women gossiped. Just appearing with Matt must have been enough to quell the questions, because no one asked me a thing. Besides, they were too busy discussing their own lives.

"We got a hot tub."

"You should see the bay windows in our new house."

"I just hope this baby is as perfect as my son Jason."

"Simon still can't ejaculate."

Matt and I danced, and I could feel every muscular inch of his body next to mine, his washboard stomach, his strong hand in the small of my back, his thighs tight from riding his bicycle to Bloomington and back, and his breath on my neck. He smelled like soap, aftershave, and chewing gum. I felt dizzy.

Later when he drove me home, he walked me to the door and kissed me once. My heart did a somersault, and I remembered how I used to study his lips in Advanced Biology.

Chapter 15

Uncle Frank

One bright, spring day when I was 14, I was home alone when I heard a knock at the door. I opened the door and found my grandfather, Paw Paw, grinning idiotically on our front porch.

"RaeAnn," he stammered.

I opened the door to let him in, and he dragged his left leg through the door, weaving. He staggered and grinned at me again. I thought he was drunk, and I was shocked because I had never seen him drunk.

"RaeAnn," he said again grinning. "Call your mom. I've had a stroke."

I called my mom at the beauty parlor. She was having her hair frosted, and they'd just pulled her hair through the cap. Her hairdresser tied a scarf around her head, and Mom rushed home, took Paw Paw to the VA hospital, called Kay, had Daddy pick up Tilly, only later remembering her hair.

I visited Paw Paw in his dull yellow room and watched him as he tried to be cavalier about his stroke. Half his face, sunk by the battle with gravity, hung tiredly. The other half was tense from keeping up appearances stood at attention. Both his eyes dared you to feel sorry for him.

He wore striped pajamas, begged me to bring him a dilly bar, and beat me at hearts unmercifully. He joked about his friend Ray, a fellow VA patient, who planned to buy the VA hospital.

"The first thing I'm going to do," Ray told Paw Paw, who told us "is go in each and every room and piss on the floor." The part Paw Paw liked best about Ray was his name, the same name as my dad's. The way he said, "Ray got in trouble for dancing through the halls naked," you'd think he was talking about my dad.

"Ray set fire to the linen closet on our floor," he told my dad. "He was sneaking a cigarette."

My dad smiled and blew air through his mustache.

When he was released from the hospital, Tilly took him home to Oldenburg to nurse him back to health. And when he was forced to let her care for him, help him with the simplest tasks, walking, taking a bath, cutting his food, the good side of his face gave up the smile, and he became bitter. Not at her, never at her. He was mad at himself.

He sat in the kitchen in his orange hospital chair by the window, fingering the cactuses I had given him through the years with his numb fingers. He didn't talk to anyone except the priest that brought him communion daily, and Tilly, who he thanked with his eyes for every deed she did ungrudgingly.

Tilly stopped having her hair done and let her hair go gray. In the span of one afternoon starting on our front porch, they both became old.

Paw Paw died a year later, but not without first learning to write and eat and walk by himself again. He sent me shaky notes that took him all day to write, reminding me to do my homework and help my mom "run the electrik broom." The month before he died, he wrote an entire letter to my sister detailing his love for her.

Paw Paw was a big man who took me riding in his yellow pickup truck to Delaware, Indiana to see his friend. At the time, I thought we were in the state of Delaware and wondered how we got there so quick. Paw Paw was a man surrounded by women who adored him and whom he cherished with his brown, winking eyes, his rough, callused hands, and his oversized heart. My dad studied under Paw Paw and became the man in the center of a life full of females, the next happiest man alive.

I memorized the love story, first of my mom and dad, and then of Tilly and Paw Paw, for I wanted my husband to be next in line.

Paw Paw worked for Furness Ice Cream driving a truck when he married Tilly. He had to hock his mother's wedding band for the money to marry Tilly and for one year, they lived in separate houses.

The birth of my mom nearly killed Chantilly, and Paw Paw had to work two jobs so that he could hire a nurse to care for his daughter and his wife. He bought Tilly a little bell that she could ring when she needed something. Even after she got better, he continued to buy her a bell every year, signifying, I supposed, his promise that he would always be a bell ring away.

The Depression marked Tilly in odd ways. For instance, she kept canned food in her basement, she stashed whiskey bottles in the bathroom closet, and she bought toilet paper and toothpaste in bulk. She'd buy six packages of toilet paper at dollar days even though she had shelves and shelves of it. I think she thought her stock of supplies perpetuated her life. "I can't die now, I still have three tubes of Colgate to use up," she might have thought.

She and Paw Paw lived in a series of houses on the Southside. "I always made him move. A couple times a year," Tilly told me. "He had to work so hard to keep me happy. Finally, I told him if he bought me a house on the Northside, I'd never ask to move again."

The doctor told Tilly that Mom would be her only child, and because back then only children were a rarity, they stressed to my mom that she didn't have any brothers or sisters because she was perfect and they needed only her. She was the only child they wanted. Paw Paw doted on my mom and would have even if she weren't the only child. He bought her teddy bears and swore she was the prettiest girl in the world.

When Paw Paw left for the war, he gave her his St. Christopher medal and a promise he'd be back as soon as he could. Mom kept the medal in a heart-shaped jewelry box in her top drawer. I have the one he wore in the War.

During the war, Tilly worked at Wasson's, and mom stayed after school with her grandma, Paw Paw's mother, where she was terrorized with butcher knives and tales of Blind Billy. Mom never forgave Tilly for her days at that house and, worse, for having my Aunt Kay the year after Paw Paw returned from the war.

"You said you only needed one daughter. I'm the only one you need," mom wailed. "You said I was perfect and you just wanted me. Aren't I perfect anymore?"

Paw Paw worked late so that he could buy both Mom and

Tilly gold bracelets, diamond rings, cashmere sweaters—anything they wanted. Tilly sewed Mom gorgeous dance dresses with sequin busts and layers of chiffon skirts. She made sure that Mom had the right shoes, gloves, and underwear.

Meanwhile, they thought Kay was too young to notice. Kay, in her cowboy boots, rode the wooden fence in the yard and waited until dark for Paw Paw to come home. She waited for him the same every evening until Tilly called her in from the porch. He worked late at his service station every night so that he could afford anything his girls wanted.

I didn't know what Tilly and Paw Paw thought of Daddy when mom came home and announced she'd gotten married at the Justice of the Peace. Paw Paw gave Daddy a job at the gas station while he wasn't in school, and he drove down to Bloomington every weekend with carloads of groceries. Though, I knew he never said in words to my Dad the way he expected his daughter to be treated and the kind of life he hoped for her, I was sure my dad got the picture. And if Paw Paw were living, I didn't think he could recall an instance when Ray let him down although there were years of tests and unspoken study.

When Lynne was born, Paw Paw added another girl to the list of women who adored him unfailingly. He bought her first diamond when she was six which she promptly lost down the drinking fountain in first grade. She kept the second one until she was 13; she lost that one playing Kick the Can in Mr. Cribbage's yard. The emerald she lost in high school, the ruby after she married.

I, on the other hand, still had my rings as well as the St. Christopher's medal. I couldn't say for sure why I was Paw Paw's favorite. Timing, probably. I came at a time when his first heart attack forced him to slow down. By the second one, he was at home entirely. Kay had long since dismounted the horse-fence and gone to college, so when Paw Paw came home this time, I was the one waiting for him. I was 7 and eager to spend my time teaching Paw Paw.

He bought me a chalkboard and a little pointer, and I taught him the alphabet in his garage. He bought a little school desk just my size from some closed down school. But of course, since

I was the teacher, it was he who sat at the little desk and wrote out his ABC's. I couldn't remember if I knew he was joking or not—about not being able to read.

The thing that scared and delighted us most about Paw Paw was that you never knew if he was joking or not. Daddy, a virtual chimney and a grown adult, acted like he didn't smoke in front of Paw Paw. He'd sneak into the driveway or down the basement or go for a car ride to have a smoke. Every year Paw Paw would wrap up a carton of cigarettes for my dad for Christmas. And every year, he'd let him open them, then take them back, saying, "This must be some mistake. You don't smoke, Ray." The next year he'd wrap up another carton, in fact it was probably the same carton the whole time. If Daddy was afraid to smoke, Mom and Aunt Kay really had to hide their habit. Even when my mom was 40 and Kay was 30, they'd hid down the basement, giggling and smoking like two school girls

Paw Paw was a big prankster and once convinced me and Sam to take a midnight walk through the nun's graveyard. Then he slipped over there the back way and laid in a grave. When I walked by, he grabbed my leg. I thought I'd met my Maker that time.

Another favorite trick was to move the kneeler from St. Joseph's church. Paw Paw kept an odd collection of things. He had a bowling pin from the old bowling alley in Brightwood, a wooden school desk from Harry S. Truman high, a billy club, and a genuine prayer kneeler. When they came down to Oldenburg, Mom and Aunt Kay liked to sneak down to King's for a drink. The minute they'd leave, Paw Paw would get up and drag the kneeler to a strategic place in their drunken paths. When they got home, we'd hear a big crash. The next morning Paw Paw would say, "Couldn't you sleep? I heard you come in last night. Did you want to wake the whole house?"

"It was Uncle Frank," Kay would say.

Uncle Frank was a ghost we called on to take the blame.

"Did Uncle Frank give you that big bruise on your knee?" he would ask.

Even though they knew each time to look for the kneeler, one of them still hit it. When Paw Paw died, Tilly gave the kneeler to my mom.

Paw Paw's favorite joke was Uncle Frank, who allegedly hung himself in the attic of the house in Oldenburg.

"When his wife opened the door, he swung down," he told me, swinging open the door and pointing to where Frank hung. "He's still around here pulling pranks. Better watch out for him."

Anytime we heard anything rattle upstairs or anytime anything missing turned up, we called on Uncle Frank.

"Who got in at 3 in the morning last night?" Mom said to Lynne.

"Must have been Uncle Frank," she said.

"Who ate the last piece of pie?" Paw Paw said.

"Uncle Frank," Daddy said, belching.

Even though I knew we didn't have an Uncle Frank, I ran by that door and never slept upstairs by myself. Sam, who had been to the house hundreds of times, was still scared to go upstairs by herself, for we never told her we didn't have an Uncle Frank.

After the wedding, I sat in Tilly's room watching her put on her face cream. Her hair was wrapped up in the usual toilet paper, keeping her beehive in place. She saw me watching.

"You know I'd make a good bug light. You could make me stand in the yard. I'd attract the bugs, and when they flew in my hair, they'd break their necks and die," she said.

I laughed. "Your skin is so beautiful. No wrinkles at all," I said.

"I never wore makeup. Not a drop of blush or eye shadow or mascara. Nothing. Although once Katie convinced me to shave off my eyebrows and pencil some in. They never grew back. That's why I don't have any eyebrows."

I was laying on the other twin bed in my sister's old room, now Tilly's. I used to be afraid to sleep by myself when I was young, so although I had my own room, my sister also had to share half of hers.

"Lynne and I used to sleep in this room together," I said. "She made me sleep closest to the door, so the boogey man would get me first."

"Want to spend the night?" Tilly said.

"Sure."

We spent the night talking about her memories. She told me her mother was never well after her younger brother Charlie was born.

"My father stepped into an elevator that wasn't there," she said. "And one of my brothers, Junior, killed himself."

We finally fell asleep. Later in the middle of the night, I rolled over, and she was staring at me.

"Your father just put peanut butter in my hair," she said.

I thought she was going crazy, like Ruthie Gilder's grandmother who went crazy and insisted someone was breaking into her house and stealing the peanut butter. They finally had to put her away when they found her cooking undershirts on the stove for lunch.

"I just dreamt your father put peanut butter in my hair," she said. "I wish I had my dream book with me. I wonder what that means."

Later that night I heard her whimpering.

"What is it?" I tried to wake her up.

"It's the man with the umbrella. Can't you see him? He's standing over there in the corner. He usually stands outside the window, but now he's in the room. Can't you see him over in the corner?" She cried. "He's coming to get me again."

Chapter 16

A Bird in the House

One night six weeks after Jessica, Lynne's daughter, was born, I couldn't sleep because I thought I was suffocating. I couldn't get enough air even though I concentrated on breathing in and out to relax. My parents had gone to Gatlinburg for the weekend and were on their way home, so I decided I was worried about them getting home.

The next morning Lynne found Jessica, her new baby, cold and hard and blue and dead in her crib. She had died from Sudden Infant Death Syndrome or "crib death." When she called me crying and said those three words, "Jessie is dead," I thought it was all a nightmare. I thought it was the end of the world. As Matt drove me over to Lynne's house, an accident happened inches in front of us. Two cars, seemingly hurled from nowhere, moved lightening-quick, uncontrollably at each other, crashed, and then moved even more quickly away. I didn't see where the cars came from, the direction they were heading, how they got in each other's way. I thought that God had thrown them from the sky aiming at me.

After Jessie was born I had stopped by the nursery to see her own last time before I left. "Where's Jessie?" I asked the nurse.

"They're giving her a bath. Do you want me to go get her?"

"No, I'll be seeing her plenty," I had said. How wrong I had been.

When we got to Lynne's house, Harry ran out the front door. I imagined that Lynne was sedated, in a drug-induced state of grief in her bed. I didn't know where I picked up the idea that they sedated people when someone died. Probably from a soap opera. It wasn't until after I hugged Harry that I heard Lynne whimpering in the kitchen.

"She was cold and hard and blue and dead," Lynne said. "She was my favorite."

We all hugged each other and cried and wondered why.

"She was the prettiest of the three," I said.

"She was my baby," Lynne said.

The day moved in slow motion, making funeral decisions, greeting family members and crying all over again, staring into space and holding on to Nadine and Caroline tight. I helped Lynne pick out an outfit for Jessie.

"We need one with a hat," she said, "because they'll have to cut her head open to perform the autopsy."

I picked out a pink one to match the pink coffin with etched flowers that Harry chose.

"Where can we bury her?" Lynne said.

"With Paw Paw," I said. "Or maybe Daddy will spring for a crypt for all of us." We laughed just a little.

"The priest suggested having her cremated," Lynne said. "Then if we move, I can take her with me. She'll always be with me then. Besides I want to be cremated."

"I didn't know that you wanted to be cremated," I said. "I want to be buried in one of those slats in a building. I don't want to be put in the ground."

"The dogs were all cremated. We have their ashes in coffee cans out in the garage."

"Where will you keep Jess's ashes?" I said.

"Maybe we could build a little shrine in the yard."

I hesitated.

"I don't want to put her in the ground," she said, crying. "Not my baby girl."

As each person arrived, Lynne looked scared and said, "Is it Daddy?" Mom and dad were still on the road. We couldn't get in touch with them at first, and when we did, Lynne ran from the phone, saying, "I can't tell Daddy. You tell him." Finally, Tilly, Mom, Daddy, Aunt Kay, and her two boys pulled in, each with paper bags full of clothes. We must have inherited an aversion to overnight bags; none of us owned one. Instead, we all packed our clothes in brown grocery bags and looked like the traveling branch of the Beverly Hillbillies.

Daddy cried on the front porch. "I never even got to change her diaper," he said.

Mom held Lynne like a baby on the couch and rocked her

back and forth. Tilly sat with the girls.

"When is Jessie coming home?" Caroline said.

"Jessie died," Nadine said. "I miss her."

"I'll be going to look after her, take care of her soon," Tilly said to me.

We scheduled the funeral as early as possible because nobody wanted to wait around, anticipating the inevitable sight of Jessica in that pink-etched coffin. The day of the funeral, we put on hose and fixed our hair and avoided each other's eyes. I watched *Dumbo* for the fifth time with the girls. I started crying before we even got to the funeral home.

When Lynne saw her baby lying in that coffin, she made a sound I would never forget—like a wounded animal. Her grief went beyond human compassion or understanding. The sound was so base, so elemental, so primitive. I knew she had been marked in the worst way—a mother who had lost her child.

I inched towards the casket to look at my niece. She looked like a porcelain doll wrapped in her pink satin blanket that I had special-ordered and had shipped from Saks. Her skin was smooth and white, like bone china from England. Her unruly hair was covered by the cap.

"I want to hold her," Lynne said.

The funeral director placed her in Lynne's arms, and Lynne smiled. As Lynne held her, I saw blood on the coffin pillow.

"She'll always be your baby," I said.

"I don't want to put her down," Lynne said. "It feels so good to hold her. I don't want to put her down."

"She'll always be your baby," I said.

The flowers and the parade of mourners were amazing, but the sadness was unspeakable. I wrote the homily for Mass:

"And when she was born, all bloody and beautiful, she cried for just one second, not longer than one good scream, for she wanted to get the fussing over with and get on with her life. Then the doctor handed her to Lynne and Harry, and they loved her and saw that she was perfect and beautiful.

"She started looking around immediately with her bright eyes. She studied the faces around her with wonderment. She reached out for her mother to touch and love her back.

Absorbing all the love, touching, understanding, living.

"She was like that her whole life, and for her lifetime, she was the center of our universe—all of us here today. We revolved around her—our little sunshine. She spent her life in someone's arms. We never set her down. Each of us fighting and waiting in line for our turn to hold and love her.

"She had the love of two wonderful, proud parents, two beautiful sisters, two sets of grandparents, two great-grandmothers, many aunts and uncles, cousins and friends—all of us here. And she had the love of God.

"Her short life was full—she rode on an airplane, she played on the beach, she saw Disney World, she met and loved many of us here. She received many gifts, but more than that she gave *us* the greatest gift of all—the love of a child.

"And when she died, it was a beautiful sunny day, and we were angry at more than just the sunshine that dared peep out on such a day. Later it rained, tears from the sky, for just a moment. Then a big, full, bright rainbow stretched in front of the house. Caroline said that Jessica had ridden that rainbow into heaven.

"When she was born, we knew the instant we saw Jessica that she was special—touched—different than us. We could see in her bright eyes and beautiful face that she was marked—an angel already."

The greatest fear I had was that I'd forget Jessica. It seemed easier, less painful, to push her out of my mind, but then I revolted at that idea. She was a part of our family, and I didn't want to forget her presence and her importance. I wanted to remember everything about her, the way her mouth made ohs, the way she blinked and studied me intently.

This second death in the death trifecta knocked us over.

"You tell Tilly she better take care of herself," Lynne said when we left. "Tell her she has to—for me."

Tilly checked in to the hospital a few days later.

"Let's not tell Lynne," I said to Mom.

"She's coming over today. What are we going to say when she asks where Tilly is?"

"We can't tell her. What if she goes off the deep end?" I said.

"We have to tell her. Anyway, she's just having her heart medication regulated."

"You know how those hospitals are. Once they get you in there, they don't let you out. I better remind Tilly."

"That's real sweet," Mom said.

I was worried about Tilly and visited her every day. Sometimes Matt went with me. She seemed in great spirits. She liked her roommate and complained about the food and her nightgown.

"I told your mom to bring me up a nice nightgown and she brought me this dish rag. I'm embarrassed to walk the halls. Plus I'm starving. I found a piece of candy in my purse, but I couldn't get the wrapper undone. So I sucked on it for a while and spit it out on the floor.

"My roommate's a real interesting one," she said. "She named all her kids after the states. She's got an Oklahoma Annie, Arizona Marie, Montana Jack, and Wyoming. Imagine that. When she told me, I said, 'What are their nicknames? The postal abbreviations?'"

Meanwhile, Mom had a mammogram. "It was like lying a canned ham up on the shelf," she said. "It was humiliating." She had a big lump of cancer removed from her back. Daddy and Mom both had their wills made out.

Death had laid us low. It loomed like a hurricane, we were all prepared to bolt down the furniture, nail shut the windows, and wait for the next blow. We all eyed each other suspiciously and prayed with hands clenched tight at night.

Tilly walked the halls in the hospital and made friends quickly in the hospital.

"You should hear them talk," she said. "They decided that a man had to have four things for them to be interested in. Sex, but not that much, money, a nice personality, and good looks. I cracked up listening to them debate all this, and I said `And what would you offer him in return?' They didn't say anything. I said, `Hell, if he had all that, he wouldn't be interested in anyone on this floor.' They about died. But imagine. Even old Wilhelma with her yellow teeth that need Ajaxing was chiming in. I couldn't believe it."

I visited Tilly every day and called her during my lunch break. She always had a story ready for me.

"Did I ever tell you about that Chrysler your Paw Paw bought?"

"No," I said.

"Well, he never had much sense with money, so when he had it, he spent it. He bought this Chrysler with all the extras, big wooden running boards, the works. Of course, he didn't have a license plate for it, so we'd get nineteen cents worth of gas and drive it in the fields. Then he couldn't make payments on it, so it was repossessed. My dad had to give him an old car to drive."

Another time she called me at home with a story. "Did I tell you that your Paw Paw was going to go on strike after Darla was born? He had to hire a nurse to take care of the baby and me, so he couldn't afford to go on strike. He had to swallow his pride and go back in. And that nurse was such a fat-ass bitch. She kept Darla at the foot of her bed and wouldn't hardly let me see her. She served Paw Paw dinner, little cafeteria scoops of everything."

Tilly talked about Paw Paw in heaven.

"He's up there with all my hot-to-trot buddies, flirting around, having a helluva good time," she said. "And here I am. I guess it could be worse. I could be locked up in some home with old farts chasing me around in wheel chairs. Playing bingo. Eating Beef-a-roni. And no beer. Oh my goodness, no beer—I am lucky," she said. "But he won't wait forever. He's up there missing me too."

I pictured Tilly and Paw Paw. How they must have looked on that first date eating sundaes. I pictured him leaving for war and remembered photographs of him in a hula skirt with brown-breasted native women standing around him. I was surprised Tilly didn't tear up the pictures. There she was worrying, and there he was hula-ing and getting tattoos. I pictured her getting mad at him and drinking warm beer.

Lately, Tilly had been frustrated with me, annoyed with a dream I had been having. I had this same dream about getting married. As I walked down the aisle, Trixie stood.

"Don't sacrifice yourself for a few cents off coupons," she said pointing at me.

I stopped and stared, but my dad dragged me to the next row.

Sam popped up. "How about the night you met the Indianapolis Rugby team? No more nights like that. Can you give them all up?"

I stumbled on.

Emma was in the next row. "I lied. He's got one the size of a cocktail weenie," she said.

Lynne jumped up. "Does he know you have a fur coat you haven't paid off? Does he know your main hobby is shopping?"

Daddy yanked me forward. In the next row, my mom stood up.

"The minute he says I do, it'll become I used to."

Tilly was in the final row, cackling.

"Remember what I told you about marriage. It's like two mules in a harness."

Usually when I turned to look at my husband-to-be, it was Conan the Barbarian in his metal underwear. Tilly said she was frustrated because I hadn't learned my lesson.

"What lesson?" I had said.

"When you know, you know."

I had the same dream that night, but as I walked by each person, they just stood up and nodded. At the end of the aisle, Tilly was standing behind the altar. I looked at my husband and smiled.

"We have a winner," she said.

Chapter 17

Together Forever

Tilly's health never got better when she was in the hospital, and she changed dramatically. She got even older. On Christmas Eve one of the nurses gave her an overdose of her medication that sent her into a downward spiral. We were never sure what happened that night, but we thought the doctor and nurses tied to Tilly to the bed until they were sure she wasn't going to die, at least not right away, and in the morning they called my mom and aunt.

"I think this is it," the doctor said.

When we got there, Tilly was thrashing and kicking and screaming in her hospital gown. Her legs were black and blue, and her hair pointed to the ceiling. She was wicked and mean. I'd never seen Tilly like that.

"The bastards tried to kill me," she screamed. "Left me for dead. Well, I'm not dead. Look at me. They beat me. They tied me down. Those fat hogs the nurses sat on me while I begged for help."

The doctor called us into the hall.

"Tilly was given an overdose of her medication," he said. "And the side effects have taken their toll. Yes, we did hold her legs down, but only so that she wouldn't hurt herself. She's been hallucinating. That's a side effect of the drug overdose."

"I haven't been hallucinating," Tilly yelled from inside her room. "You're nothing but a fat old toad, and your mother should be embarrassed to have a child like you."

"We didn't expect for her to make it," the doctor said. "In fact, she's probably not going to make it more than one or two days. That's my prediction. We can make her comfortable here."

We nodded and went to see our Tilly.

"Come here RaeAnn," Tilly said to me. "I know you. I can trust you. Look what they did to me." Tilly showed me her bruised arms. "They beat me," she said and then began to cry. "You do something. Do something for me, okay? Investigate. Find out the truth. I don't want to say too much because the room is bugged."

My mom smirked.

"Damn you Darla," Till said. "I don't expect for you to believe me. I don't expect any one of you to think I'm telling the truth. But I'm old, and they treat old people like shit here. You can't believe what goes on. You can't imagine. The night before my roommate couldn't take her pill. She wanted them to crush it up and give it to her with some food. No, they crammed it down her throat and when she started gagging, they shoved it down a little further. Finally her family came in, and they acted all sweety-nicey. They hate us old people. They want to kill us."

"Get some rest," my mom said.

"I want my shot," Tilly said. "Give me my shot."

The nurses came in and gave Tilly a shot of Demerol to calm her down. She screamed and all her muscles twitched as they shot her in the leg.

For the rest of her hospital stay, my mom kept a vigil by Tilly's bed. She made the hospital staff put a cot in her room, and when they said there wasn't room for the cot, Mom slept in the chair.

"She's going to get better. I know it," Mom said.

"She's going to die," my Aunt Kay said.

We got another alert. My mom called me from the hospital to tell us Tilly was dying. We rushed to Tilly's side again. She had no blood pressure, her liver was failing, her kidney was failing, and she was hooked up to an oxygen machine. The priest came to give her Last Rites. The doctor said she wouldn't last through the hour.

That hour every one of us sat by her bedside and breathed for her. I felt as if I stopped breathing, she would. As I sat and looked at what Tilly had become, I was deeply sad. I didn't know what was best. Each breath, I thought, let her die, let her live, let her die, let her live. She had sores from being in the bed, and she looked like nothing but bones. To keep her arm from bleeding, they tied a plastic garbage sack around her hand. Her eyes were caked shut.

I was afraid to be in the room when her breathing stopped. But I was also afraid not to be in the room when her breathing stopped. I was scared. We were all scared and took turns keeping her company.

During my breaks, Matt sat with me in the hospital cafeteria. "Do you remember Paw Paw?" I asked Matt. "My grandfather?"

He nodded.

"Paw Paw would pretend he didn't know how to read," I said talking more to myself than to Matt. "I'd teach him. He'd sit in this little wooden school chair, and I'd write on the blackboard he bought me. After playing school, he'd rock me to sleep in this saggy hammock. Him in that little chair. Me in the hammock.

"He had had a heart attack and couldn't work. I remember when I was eight I was too young to visit him on the hospital floor, but they made an exception and let him come down to the lobby to see me. We played Hearts. Later when he was better, he'd watch me all day in the summer and during school he'd pick me up in his big white Oldsmobile and take me to swim practice. 'Here's some change to get a beer after workout,' he said.

"Sometimes we'd drive to the airport and watch the planes land or go visit some of his buddies. Then we'd stop at Dairy Queen and get a dilly bar. A bag of dilly bars. We'd come home and put on our aprons and run the 'electric broom,' that's what he called it. We'd cook pork chops. He taught me how to make gravy. Measure in the flour, stir it up with the grease, add the milk. We'd pick Tilly up at work, eat dinner and then spend the rest of the evening playing penny poker."

Matt took a bite of his cafeteria cheeseburger and let me talk.

"Paw Paw would have me tickle his back with a big long scratcher and comb his hair and put it in pony tails. That's when I wanted to be a hairdresser. When I wanted to be a banker, he brought home ledger receipts. I sat at my desk, my bank drive-through window, and kept detailed records of my customers withdrawals and deposits. When I wanted to be a nurse, he gave me his medical history. I wrote it down on a clipboard. Diabetes, hardening of the arteries, high blood pressure. He'd buy me a present on my sister's birthday.

I started to cry a little. Matt didn't say anything.

"Paw Paw gave Lynne a letter this Christmas telling her he loved her. 'You may think I have a favorite,' he said. 'But I love you all the same. It's just hard for me to tell you that I love you very much.' I found the letter in Lynne's jewelry box.

"I didn't get a letter," I said.

"You don't need one," Matt answered. "Come on."

"Where are we going?"

"To get some dilly bars."

First, Tilly wasn't going to last the hour, then the day. Then the next day. On the third day, she told me she was thirsty. Aunt Kay gave her some water and then wiped her dry teeth with a wash cloth, and Tilly bit her.

"You know how she hates having someone in her face," Mom said. We laughed.

The next week we took Tilly home from the hospital, and she went to her brother's daughter's wedding. She was the old Tilly. I felt like I was with the godfather—the way everyone came over and paid their respects. Tilly sat there, proud and beautiful and sipped a Bloody Mary.

"Look at them," she whispered to me. "Staring at me as if I'm some witch. Like I've come back from the dead."

"Well, you have," I said.

"I know it," Tilly said and smiled. "And I came back for a reason. I came back to tell everyone how terrible old people are treated. Don't you forget it."

"I won't."

That night she was propped up in her own bed. I sat next to her. She asked me "How do I look girl?"

"You look great."

"Don't lie to me girl," she said and closed her eyes. "When I was out of it, there was this line, and I wanted to step over it. I kept trying to step over it, but someone was holding me back. Probably your mother. Every time I got my toe over the line, I heard music. I was so tired that I wanted to die. I wanted to cross that line and hear that music. But something brought me back."

I imagined the grip that Tilly must have on life, the grip that had maintained her through all kinds of losses, the grip that even two brushes with death could not knock loose. In my heart, I also knew that she wanted to let go, but didn't know how.

"Don't be sad," she said. And I knew what she meant. I started to cry. "You'll be OK. Don't be sad."

She died two nights later at home, with Mom and Aunt Kay by her side. There was a big bolt of lightening, she took her last breath, and she died. I thought of it as God personally giving her the call. The man with the umbrella finally got her.

At the showing, the first thing I thought of when I walked in was how happy she'd be to see the crowd. I think the entire town of Oldenburg, plus all her friends and relatives—at least those that were still living—were there. All three of Aunt Kay's husbands were there.

"The flowers are spectacular," I said to no one in particular.

I picked the farthest corner from the casket, and as Tilly would say, I "held court." I remembered that Tilly would tell me if I was somewhere I didn't want to be, or if I wasn't having fun, to pretend she was there to talk to. "Think of all the funny things we'd be laughing about," she'd said. "Act like you're having the time of your life, and then you will be."

I watched all her buddies go up to the coffin and pay their respects. I knew it was mainly sad for them because they were thinking that they might be next. I went to the bathroom and found Aunt Kay smoking a cigarette.

"Isn't it awful out there?" she said. "I've got a cooler in the truck. I can't wait to pop one. I know Mom sure the hell wouldn't mind. "

"She's probably wishing she had one right now. You know how she hated people breathing on her. It made her gag."

"Did you see the dinky flowers Paw Paw's brother sent?

That big blow mouth is loaded, and he sends this piece of shit planter. Did you see it?"

"I haven't looked at all the flowers."

She put out her cigarette, and we both headed back out. I went to my corner and surveyed the room. Look at Old Lady Donlovey, I thought to Tilly. Waltzing around, hanging on Duke's every word. His wife Cecile died, you know. You should have thought of that earlier. Scoping funeral parlors for eligible. At least Paw Paw went before you. If it were him Old Lady Donlovey was pawing after, I think you'd sit up and throw Uncle Petey's cheap planter right at her head.

I smiled thinking how amused Tilly would be to hear me say all this. When Tilly would get really tickled, she'd throw her head all the way back and laugh. As if the laugh physically knocked her back. I could picture Tilly laughing really hard, until tears rolled out the corner of her eyes. Tears started pooling in my eyes.

And when she'd cry, she'd stick her rolled up tongue out. Anytime she'd get upset, she'd stick her tongue out, and I'd know she was getting ready to cry. Nadine did the same thing.

I started to cry. After everyone left, I went into the showing room and inched my way up to the casket.

"You look really nice, Tilly," I said. "So peaceful. The beehive is perfect."

I lightly touched her hair. Then her hands. Tilly used to sew the most beautiful clothes. She made Lynne and I pinafores and smock tops with watermelons or kangaroos sewed on for pickets. She made us Raggedy Ann and Andy dolls with "I love you" embroidered in a heart on their chests. When she broke her arm, and it didn't mend right, she had to quit sewing. She described to me dresses she would have liked to have made for Lynne's girls. She had wanted to make my wedding dress. I stood there running my finger along her worn hand, crying.

"Chantilly lace and a pretty face," I said.

I that Tilly had to teach me to take the step forward in our family—to become an active participant instead of just a listener. It was my job to realize the importance of family, to become the family historian and pass down the traditions, to remind everyone all we really had was each other, to keep us together. I realized a family was a fragile thing, easily broken. We had to remember to cherish each other, treat each other gently.

I knew that Tilly wanted me to not only be loved, but to love back myself. I could love my family easily, there was no threat in that, but I had to venture out—love someone for myself and make our love story an example that generations to come could look to. And I knew who that person was. Falling in love wasn't a game, like I thought. It wasn't something you could set out on a mission for, something you could make happen. Falling in love was something you had to trust in.

I knelt at the kneeler, put my head down, and sobbed until Daddy tapped me on the shoulder. He hugged me—one of his back-breaking-I-am-the-saddest-happiest-man-alive hugs. Mom, Lynne, and Aunt Kay stood in the doorway bawling.

I wrote the eulogy that night.

"Tilly's greatest worry was that she wasn't needed anymore. 'No one needs me' she said. And maybe she was right. She had spent her entire life teaching us. 'Keep your shoulders back.' 'Sit up straight.' 'Smile.' She was our advisor, our role model, our source of wisdom, our coach. She taught us how to be ourselves. And maybe it seemed as if we'd reached a point where we didn't need her. Maybe she had taught us enough.

"But that can't be true. I have so many questions I want to ask her. There's so much more I need to know. There so much more I want to tell her. I wake up today and ask 'Where is my Tilly? Where is my Tilly?'

"I want her back.

"But in wanting her back, I am being the one thing that she was not—selfish. In wanting her back, I am thinking only of myself. I'm not thinking of her.

"For I know that she must be happy. She is reunited with those that loved her before we did. Her dad Fred and mother Adele. Her sister Katie and brothers Junior and Vern. Her great granddaughter. And most of all her husband Elmer. Surely he must be saying 'At last, at last, together at last.'

"And I know that—we all know that—she will never truly be gone. She will be in our hearts and our lives and our memories. She has shaped each of us—daughters, brother, granddaughters, great grandchildren, sons-in-law, friends. She has give us our own special gifts. Our love for her will always remain.

"And we remain. Look around. This is what Tilly has left us. This is what she taught us. You always have your family. Sisters and brothers. Mothers and daughters. Fathers and sons. Husbands and wives. This is the strength—the gift—she left us.

"This is the gift we must carry on."

At the graveyard, I stayed by myself and sat on Paw Paw's tombstone.

"So you're with your great love now, Til. Finally got a man, and you promised you'd never leave me. I can still feel you soaring around here somewhere, like a bird. Calling purty-girl to Nadine and Caroline."

Their plot was shaded by a big tree, and I wondered whether Tilly would be angry that she wasn't out in the sunshine.

"Do you miss me? I know you must. Even with Paw Paw there, you must still miss me. All I keep thinking of is how much I miss you and will keep on missing you."

Looking at the cold, hard, ugly brown hole carved out of the ground, and smelling the sickening sweet smell of flowers, I cried some more and felt sorry for myself. I ran my finger along the newly chiseled tombstone. Chantilly and Elmer. Together forever.

When I looked up, I saw my intended standing by his beat up car. He handed me a bunch of tissues and opened the car door.

"I love you Matt," I said.

He smiled. "I know."

Matt and I drove back to my house. Everyone was staying at our medium-size, three bedroom house. Lynne and Harry drove the motor home over. Last night Mom and Daddy slept in their room, and Ernie and Kay in mine. The two girls slept in Tilly's room, and Kay's two boys slept in the living room. Harry, Lynne, two dogs, and I slept in the motor home.

"Stop by," I told Matt. "My bedroom is right in the middle of the street now, so I'll be out front in my pajamas directing traffic. Just honk if I'm not out there."

Another dog slept inside and kept my mother awake all night. He kept nudging her with his nose, and she kept feeding him Snickers bars from my dad's stash.

The motor home was parked on the street in front of our house. Harry set up two wire X-pens for the dogs in the front yard. Kay's truck was there along with the four family cars. My dad had moved the grill, the picnic table, and Nadine's rocking horse into the front yard because the backyard was impenetrable. It looked like we were having a party.

My Uncle Ernie and Daddy stopped at the liquor store and decided it would be best to get a keg. They were setting it up on the front porch as we pulled up. Harry had started the grill, so after my dad set the keg up, he donned his apron, hung his Coleman lantern on a tree limb and stood in the front yard grilling hamburgers. We also had coleslaw, potato salad, chips, pickles, baked beans. Tilly had just died, and we were having a picnic.

Ernie, Sam, Kay, and I played euchre.

"Hearts," I said.

"Hearts. Why'd you call it hearts?" Kay yelled.

"A little bird told me to call it hearts," I said.

"Well, maybe that little bird should be your partner," she said. "I don't like being your partner. You're too reckless."

Even with the lantern, my dad couldn't see to cook the hamburgers, so the first batch were black, crunchy lumps of charcoal, and the second batch were raw in the middle. Aunt Kay ate a raw one.

"It won't hurt you," she said. "Tilly used to say they were good for you."

"And she's dead," Ernie said.

We were all quiet as I shuffled the cards.

"I almost forgot," Kay said.

"It does seem as if she's around here," I said. "I don't know why I called it hearts last time."

"Hoyle."

I smiled. Matt and Daddy were in the kitchen making bologna sandwiches.

"I live on bologna," my dad said.

"It looks like you're underfed," my mom said and patted his big beer belly.

Harry came in. "One of the dogs got loose. Lynne get some car keys, and let's go find him. Come on," he said.

"Lynne's busy," Mom said. "Find him yourself."

"Lynne," Harry called.

"Why'd you bring those damn dogs anyway?" Mom said.

"I wanted to bring those damn dogs," Lynne said, coming down the steps. "Don't yell at Harry. I just put the girls down. Be quiet."

"I'm not yelling at him. I simply want to know why your husband brought dogs to my mother's funeral."

Harry, meanwhile, had found the car keys and left with my dad to look for the missing dog.

"I brought my dogs to my grandmother's funeral because I wanted to."

"Look, they're repeating themselves now," I said. "Quit arguing."

"Mind your own business," they both yelled back, and Nadine started crying.

"See what you've done," Lynne said to all of us.

"Tell her to cry harder. Tell her you can't hear her," I said.

Lynne glared at me and went upstairs. A couple seconds later, we heard her scream, and we ran upstairs to investigate.

"What is it?" I asked.

"A mouse. There's a mouse in that trap," she said, pointing to the corner.

"A mouse in my room?" I yelled. "I thought they lived in Tilly's room."

"They must miss her, so they moved in here," Mom said.

We all studied the mouse trap and the mouse.

"It's not dead," Aunt Kay said.

"It just got his tail caught," I said.

"Daddy," Lynne called.

"He went with Harry."

154

"Matt," I yelled. "Matt come quick."

Matt came upstairs.

"What?"

I pointed.

"It's not dead," he said.

"Kill him," Lynne said.

"Kill him," Aunt Kay agreed.

"No," I said. "We can't kill her. Let it loose."

"RaeAnn, do you want a mouse living in the house?" Lynne asked.

"He'll go out and get all his relations, and we'll have the entire crew here," Mom said. "We have to kill him."

"Think she's got a family?" I said.

"Why do you keep saying she?" Aunt Kay said.

"I don't know, but remember Tilly said she was going to come back as a mouse," I said.

Everyone looked at me like I was nuts.

"Just set her free," Lynne said finally.

"She's right. Let's set her free," Aunt Kay said.

Matt picked up the trap and carried it with the dangling mouse to the backyard. We all went outside, and Matt set the trap on the edge of our yard. He released the spring, and the mouse shook himself off and stood there.

"Born free," I sang. "As free as the wind blows."

"It won't leave."

"Try this. Ladybug, ladybug, fly away home. Your house is on fire, and you're children are alone."

The mouse lingered.

"Sing some more. That will scare him off," Kay said.

I thought and then started to sing. "Chantilly Lace, and a pretty face."

Aunt Kay joined in. "A pony tail hanging down."

"A wiggle when you walk, and a giggle when you talk," Mom sang.

"Makes the word go round," Lynne chimed in.

We all sang. "There ain't nothing in the world like a big-eyed girl, make you act so funny, want to spend my money, makes me feel real loose, like a long-neck goose, awwwww, baby, that's what I like."

I looked at Matt. "Do you think I sing pretty?"

"Yep," he said. "Beautiful."

"Gotta be love," Aunt Kay said.

"True love."

I realized then that to my family, I was beautiful. And what they thought and believed was, of course, indisputable.

About The Author

Shelley O'Hara is a freelance writer. Although this is her first novel, she has written over 90 books, mostly dealing with how to use a computer. She has a BA in English from the University of South Carolina (home of the fighting Gamecocks) and a MA in English from the University of Maryland. She lives in Indiana with her husband, son, and English Bulldog, Jelly Roll. She is working on her second book called tentatively "How to Fall in Love with Your Husband."